Learning to Love

Yasmin Peace Series Book 4

YASMIN PEACE SERIES

BOOK 1

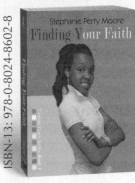

ISBN-13: 978-0-8024-8602-8

BOOK 2

ISBN-13: 978-0-8024-8603-5

BOOK 3

ISBN-13: 978-0-8024-8604-2

Join Yasmin Peace on her journey through this series
for real girls in real life with real issues.

Also Available:
The Payton Skky series and *The Carmen Browne* series

1-800-678-8812 • MOODYPUBLISHERS.COM

Learning to Love

Stephanie Perry Moore

MOODY PUBLISHERS
CHICAGO

Yasmin Peace Series Book 4

All Scripture quotations are taken from the King James Version.

Editor: Kathryn Hall
Interior Design: Ragont Design
Cover Design and Photography: Trevell Southhall at TS Design Studios
Author Photo: Bonnie Rebholz

Library of Congress Cataloging-in-Publication Data

Moore, Stephanie Perry.
    Learning to love / Stephanie Perry Moore.
       p. cm. — (Yasmin Peace series ; bk. 4)
    Summary: Fourteen-year-old Yasmin continues to rely on prayer as
her family adjusts to her father's return from jail, both of her brothers
face difficulties, her relationship with Myrick intensifies, and she fails
to get on the school dance team with her best friends.
    ISBN 978-0-8024-8605-9
    [1. Family problems—Fiction. 2. Fathers—Fiction. 3. Christian
life—Fiction. 4. High schools—Fiction. 5. Schools—Fiction.
6. Brothers and sisters—Fiction. 7. Triplets—Fiction. 8. African
Americans—Fiction.] I. Title.

PZ7.M788125Le 2009
[Fic]—dc22

                                                        2009009126

                          1 3 5 7 9 10 8 6 4 2

Printed in the United States of America

Dedicated to
2009 Delta Beaus
Brandon D.Steward Abernathy
Elijah Shabazz Cotton
Demetrius De'ante' Collins
Bennard Quinton Franklin
Brent Abington Gills
Victor Jaymes Johnson
Wynton Deonte' Jamari Jordan
Christopher Keith Mitchell
Taurean Mitchell Stevenson
Travis Maurice Stuart Jr.
Martavius Charles Thompson
George Douglas Waits
Kenneth Alexander Worthy

presented by
Henry County Alumnae Chapter
Delta Sigma Theta Sorority, Inc.

What a blessing it was to present you all to society.
Seeing you all grow into true gentlemen warmed my soul.
I pray you and every person who reads this book learns that life is
about feeling, giving, and loving! Go soar and love hard.
Your dreams are waiting on you!

Contents

Chapter 1   Protector from Harm   9

Chapter 2   Better Next Time   25

Chapter 3   Happier Days Ahead   41

Chapter 4   Encourager Shines Through   55

Chapter 5   Never Stay Down   67

Chapter 6   Braver and Stronger   81

Chapter 7   Freer Hearts Abound   95

Chapter 8   Tighter Bonding Rings   107

Chapter 9   Defeater Doesn't Win   119

Chapter 10   Nurturer Stays Involved   131

Chapter 11   After Total Security   145

Chapter 12   Healer Provided Love   157

Acknowledgments   171

Discussion Questions   174

Chapter 1

Protector
from Harm

At fourteen years old, I already knew about the stresses of life. However, I wasn't going to let the tough times beat me. I am a survivor; after all I'm from the hood. Someway, somehow I was going to find a way to love every part of my dysfunctional world. As I had learned from my middle school mentors, you have to look at life from a positive perspective.

Since it was Labor Day weekend, I was excited to be outside at the hopping neighborhood block party. So much had been happening in my crazy world. Yes, I had lost a brother to suicide over a year ago, and I miss him a lot. But things were finally looking up. Yeah! After six long years of being behind bars, my dad was out at last. Now he's a truck driver and lives near us in Jacksonville, Florida.

My brothers and I were glad to finally have Dad's strong presence in our lives. We would just have to learn how to love each other as a normal family again and find a way for our loss to make us stronger.

Also, my mom now has a steady job. She's not struggling and trying to make ends meet by working at dead-end jobs like she used to do. She still works hard, but having a career as a medical technician makes her feel worthy.

My two brothers, York and Yancy, and I are triplets. And they're still acting crazy. No one could tell stubborn York anything. And though Yancy is smart, he hasn't really been applying himself. He thinks he knows it all anyway. My folks were getting stressed with them acting out, so they decided they'd work together and stay on their sons.

My best friend, Myrek, and I are into each other. The guy who I now could admit had my heart was back in my life. He and I are about to meet up down the street.

"Hey, cutie pie," he said as he saw me approach the corner.

We used to live right next door to each other, but since our apartment caught on fire, we had to move to the other side of the complex. Jacksonville in September is still pretty hot, and to be outside at night on a long weekend—let's just say our projects were jammin'.

"Okay, so why you got that basketball?" I asked him, knowing that Myrek loved to play and hoping that he wasn't changing our plan to spend time together. I picked up on the clue that he wanted to go and play ball with the guys in our hood.

"Your brothers were just telling me about this little tournament going on against that wack team around the way," he explained. I knew that he was trying to justify why he was thinking about doing something different.

So I put my hands on my hips and said, "Come on now. We supposed to be doing our thing."

He came up to me and said playfully, "Tell me, how were we gonna kick it today?"

"I guess you'll never find out if you're gonna be playing basketball." Pouting, I turned around and started walking back toward my place.

"Oh, see now, why you gotta do me like that?" He jogged around to the front of me and tossed the ball at me. The hard ball just missed hitting me in my nose.

"Ow!" I screamed extra loud.

"I'm sorry! I'm sorry!"

I swatted at him. "See, you tryna play!"

"I'm trying to play with you," he smiled and said, realizing I was actually okay.

All of a sudden, York and Yancy came up full speed behind me. Yancy almost knocked me down and thought he was being funny. I rolled my eyes at them both. Couldn't they see that I wanted time with Myrek?

"Quit bothering the brother. Let him have a little fun with his boys. Man, y'all just got back together and you already smothering him," York scolded.

The three of them stood there waiting for a reaction out of me. My crazy brother York was really starting to get on my nerves. I wanted to take my foot and kick him in the knee so that he would fall down and run back home crying or something.

But, realistically, I couldn't believe he was gonna call me out like that. He knew how much I had been tussling, wrestling, and all upset that Myrek was dating some other new chick at our school. This girl, Raven, had given me much drama by rubbing it all in my face because she and Myrek were an item. I had tried to push it off like he really didn't matter and act like he was just my friend. But the closer I saw them getting and the more I saw him with somebody else, it really touched my heart that—you know what?—that was my place in his life. I mean, at least we had to give us a try. Myrek had wanted that for so long, but I was the one running in a completely opposite direction.

It was probably because of all the problems we'd been having. And besides, our parents were dating, which could be another complication. Well, now that situation was on rocky ground. My brothers and I secretly hoped that our parents would get back together. But knowing how much distance there had been between the two of them—was that even possible?

"Earth to Yasmin." Myrek interrupted my thoughts. "Hello, hello?"

"What? You wanna go play with them?" I said as I saw him looking at me with puppy-dog eyes. "Then, go play!"

But Myrek turned to the boys and declared, "All right, she's got an attitude, y'all. I'ma stay with my girl."

"Man, you know we can't beat them without you," Yancy pleaded with Myrek and York stood silently backing him up.

It was so cool because my brothers hadn't been getting along. But then the whole fire incident happened and that brought them closer. It was a pretty rough experience. York had gone into our next door neighbor's apartment to help her get out of the flames. Yancy had felt bad and wanted to go in after him. I don't know, but when York came out alive, something changed for us. Maybe it was because we had already lost our oldest brother, Jeff; I guess we all just knew that, as hard as life was, it's a blessing to have each other. So we were learning how to get along and how to care about one another. We were beginning to understand that other people's feelings mean something.

Giving up on convincing Myrek to go along, my brothers went on down the street. I could tell Myrek really wanted to play when he kept fumbling with that stupid ball.

There would be plenty of times for us to be together and have fun. And I did care about his thoughts. So I said, "You know what? I'm just gonna head home. You can play."

Immediately, he got overly excited. "For real? I can play?" Then, without further hesitation, he said, "Come on. I'ma walk you back home."

"What you mean, you gonna walk me back home? I want to watch," I said, frowning like he wanted to keep me away from the action. Actually, I had just decided to change my mind.

"It's not gonna be nobody but dudes out on the court. You and me can hang out tomorrow. I just don't want you hanging around like that. They talk about girls that just hang out and stuff. Mm-mm, not my girl."

"Your girl? Wow. That sounds pretty good," I said to him.

"You look pretty good."

We walked hand in hand back to my place and it just felt so special. We hadn't agreed much in the past but now we were together. When we stepped onto my porch, he pulled me closer to him. I knew that he was about to kiss me. Just then my dad pulled into the driveway and shined his lights on both of us. We jerked away from each other.

Dad got out of his car quicker than if the engine was on fire and rushed up to us. "Hey, what's going on here! What is this?"

"Dad, you know Myrek," I said.

"I don't think I know this Myrek because the Myrek I knew was your buddy. Son, what's going on? You all up close on my daughter. I ain't having none of that, young man. Uh-uh. And you'd better know it!"

Myrek was shaking. "I-I was just telling her good night, sir."

"Well, you don't need to tell her good night . . . blowing your bad breath all on her and everything—"

"Dad!" I said, hot that my father was ruining our time.

"Seriously," he scolded, "y'all need to step back and always have three to four feet between y'all. If you can't do that, y'all don't need to be in the same space. You got it? And another thing, y'all are still too young to be dating anyway."

"Dad!" I shouted again.

"I got you, sir," Myrek said, quickly giving my dad respect. "Yas, I'll holla at you later." And he jogged off.

"I know he just told me what I wanted to hear. I'm gonna talk to your mama about this."

"Dad!" I said a little softer this time, "he's my boyfriend."

But he was truly mad and said, "So you say. But your dad, whose opinion counts, says no way!"

⋘◈⋙

Other than my dad embarrassing me and the trouble I went through with Myrek's ex-girlfriend, the school year had really gotten off to a pretty good start. I liked all my teachers, and the class work in high school wasn't too hard so far. And in spite of Dad's opposition to it, Myrek and I had our thing and, whatever that thing was, we were straight.

Besides all of that, my relationship with Veida, Asia, and Perlicia was now very cool. In middle school Perlicia and Asia had always gotten up under my skin. And Veida had betrayed my family. But thankfully, at the very end of that year, we had worked through all those difficulties.

I realized that all three girls weren't much different from me. I mean, we all had some type of problems at home. At first, I thought Veida didn't know what hard times were because her father was a lawyer and she lived in a huge house with her entire family. Her older sister was a senior this year and she really had it going on. But even though all that seemed right, her parents had some issues. Veida's dad was so busy with his legal practice that he wasn't paying enough attention to his home life. So everything wasn't so happy after all.

I wasn't expecting it but Veida got into a relationship with one of my brothers. Then the next thing I knew she started liking the other one. She also still liked a boy named Maurice from her old middle school. He went to high school with us too. Through all of that Veida became troubled. Her feelings were confused, and that led her to cause a lot of drama in my family. But, at the end of the day, she felt really bad about it all and now she's my girl again. We just vowed to be friends for real. We were not only modeling buddies who wanted to look good on the outside, but also girls who had each other's backs and would help each other build up our self-esteem.

Perlicia, on the other hand, was really a loudmouth. She wasn't polished around the edges. Maybe I could help her with that. She and I are gonna have to talk more seriously and really get closer. Our friendship should mean more than just being around each other because we both were popular.

And then there's my girl, Asia. Her mom was in a relationship and the guy came on to Asia. For the longest time, her mom didn't believe her. Thankfully, that was all resolved and her mom kicked the guy to the curb. But that crazy situation took its toll on Asia and her mom's relationship. Then Asia was trying to date this guy who was also a senior. She got in a little over her head when the guy wanted her to go farther than she was ready to go. She told me that she was done with him, so hopefully she left all of that alone. But she and I need to talk about that too.

"Come on, come on! We gotta get in there and get a good seat!" Asia said as she pulled my arm to catch up with Perlicia and Veida. The four of us were going to the dance team tryouts meeting. Being a Trojanette dance girl made freshman stock go up dramatically. There were twenty slots on the team: five seniors, five juniors, five sophomores, and five freshmen. The first fifteen positions had been filled the year before. So there were only five spots open. There must have been at least sixty girls in the gym who were salivating at the mouth, wishing and wanting desperately to be on the team.

The Trojanettes performed three numbers for the rest of us. We were gonna have to learn the numbers in a week. Those girls were sassy, sharp, and all that; just seeing their routines made me very intimidated. I've always danced around the house, but I definitely haven't had any real training or anything like that. Veida had taken ballet and tap for years, and Perlicia and Asia had been in a hip-hop class at a recreation center for a long time.

"Hello, ladies. I'm Gloria Smith, the dance team sponsor. As you can see, the Trojanettes are awesome. We come with it. We perform with excellence. And we get respect. We're looking for five girls who possess the pizzazz, skill, wit, and charm to join us. We want girls who can come right in and be an asset to our team. So, come on out here and try to learn this first number."

I didn't want to get up out of my seat. I loved what I saw before me, but somewhere deep within I had no confidence to accomplish it. I couldn't dance like that.

"Come on," Veida said as she yanked me up.

"Yeah, we need to get up front so we can see," Asia added.

The front? I thought. *I need to be way in the back.*

I went and stood out there with Perlicia, Asia, and Veida. But when they got comfortable in the front, I eased my way to the back. I hadn't realized, though, that I didn't get on the very back row. And I was actually standing in front of Raven and her girl, Shay. Now I was even more intimidated.

"I can't believe he chose her over me," Raven started telling her friend.

I just kept my cool and stayed focused on what I was trying to learn. According to Myrek, Raven was really bitter. But I couldn't help but wonder if she could dance.

When I started dancing, I heard Shay say, "I don't know, girl. She's basically got two left feet. She's tall and she's all right, but she ain't nowhere near as cute and tight as you and me. You can tell she doesn't have any kind of dance training like you and me. Don't worry; she won't be making this dance team."

"Okay now, let me see you do it," Ms. Smith said as she walked toward me. I really had no clue what to do. "Sweetheart, if you plan to make this team you are going to have to practice at home and really pay attention. I know we're moving fast; that's why we need girls who already have dance experience. You've just got to work hard if this is something that you want. If it doesn't work out, you can always try out next year. A lot of girls who don't make it on the freshman team try out their sophomore year and bump some of the girls off the squad."

Then she patted me on the back condescendingly and walked away. What was I supposed to take from that? Was she trying to tell me that I was not gonna make the team? Did I just need to walk off and quit right on the spot? I was so frustrated, and it didn't help that I could hear the giggles behind me. I wanted to turn around and whack somebody. But instead I took three deep breaths and stayed in my element. I was trying to concentrate on the girls teaching the first number. The only thing I could do was give it my best to learn the part.

⁓

The practice was over about an hour later. Asia, Perlicia, and Veida came over to me as soon as we were dismissed. As we headed toward our lockers, they were chatting about how easy the moves were. I was so frustrated.

Veida said, "So, what's going on with you? Why weren't you right beside us? We got this down, girl. We're planning to practice a few more minutes before it's time to go home. Let's change real fast and meet right back out here."

Trying to be realistic, I said, "I don't think I want to do this, y'all."

"What do you mean, you don't wanna do this?" Asia said to me.

"I don't have it like you guys do."

"We can teach you," Veida chimed in.

"Yeah, girl. All you gotta do is work a little harder to the beat and you'll make the squad. We checked it out and there wasn't a lot of competition. Most of those girls need to go home and try again—like never." Perlicia laughed, feeling really proud of herself.

The three of them slapped hands. They didn't understand that I was in that boat. I was nowhere near a dance expert. To make things worse, Raven and Shay walked up beside me and called themselves imitating me. I lost my balance and fell into my friends.

"Y'all really need to help your girl stay on her feet," Raven taunted.

"I know you ain't talkin', Raven. You were hiding in the back somewhere," Perlicia replied as she helped me to my feet.

Raven and Shay just laughed and walked away. I was very upset. I was a horrible dancer.

"I can't do this, y'all."

"Girl, don't even let her get to you," Asia said.

"She's just jealous about Myrek," Veida commented.

"I can go and take care of them chicks right now," Perlicia said as she took her fist, jammed it into her hand, and pushed it into me. "She don't know us."

I said, "Yeah, but they were back there with me and I wasn't that good. Okay?"

"We've got a week to practice," Veida encouraged.

All of a sudden, some girls came running out of the gym toward us yelling, "It's a fight! It's a fight!"

Seeing somebody go at it wasn't particularly where my mind was. I still needed to figure out if I should keep trying out for the dance team. Who would be crazy enough to be fighting after school anyway? Then it hit me; my brothers were trying out for basketball. Veida's ex-boyfriend, Maurice, was trying out too. That sounded like a recipe for trouble. I just knew somebody from the Peace family had gotten into something. And they probably couldn't get themselves out of it without me there to intercede. So I took off running toward the boys' gym with my three girls right behind me.

When we got there, sure enough, I couldn't see exactly what was going on because a crowd of kids were gathered around. But I heard York's voice confronting somebody. "What's up, man? You gon' call my dad a jailbird and think I ain't gonna take care of that?"

"You gon' be joining him if you don't back off!" It was Maurice for sure.

York kept challenging. "All you doing is talkin', man. I punched you and you ain't done nothin'. Your little words can't hurt me, punk. Talkin' about my daddy. Wanna be a man? Talk about me. Do something to me. Hit me! I got this. I can take care of you right here, right now."

I could hear York clearly, but I didn't know where Myrek and Yancy were until a minute later when they showed up. As always, the word about a fight had traveled fast. "What's going on?" Yancy asked me.

"It's our brother. He's trying to defend Dad's honor."

As soon as she saw Yancy, Veida started melting. "Hey, how have you been?" she asked him.

"Ugh, we don't even have time for that," I said to her.

I pulled Myrek and Yancy over to the side. "Look, York is up there fighting."

"That ain't good because he's got a knife," Yancy reported.

"What?" I was shocked at that bit of news.

"Yeah. When we were dressing out, I saw it," Myrek added. "I tried to get him to leave it in the locker, but he put it in his sock.

What's all this about anyway? Why is he up there fighting? He had a good practice. The coach really likes him."

"Well, maybe you need to go and stall the coach so that he doesn't come in here and kick my brother off the team before he even gets on," I said to Myrek.

"Yeah, partner, that's a good idea. I got York," Yancy followed up.

York certainly was a hothead. He thought the only way to prove that he had it going on was to be violent with anyone who threatened him. And, honestly, he couldn't have learned that from my father because Dad never said that the only way to be a man is to knock somebody out. In fact, it was just the opposite. He taught us through his letters and the visits we had with him that the bigger person always bows out of a fight.

It was that crazy Bone. He's the one who had been putting weird ideas into York's head. To gain respect in our community, my brother thought the only thing that he could do was hang with the neighborhood thug. And that extreme thinking was about to get him locked up for sure.

When Myrek walked off, I turned to Veida and Perlicia, "We've got to figure out a way to get rid of these people and help break up this fight. I've got to get to my brother."

"I can handle it," Perlicia responded. Then all of a sudden she yelled, "The cops are coming!" Immediately everybody started scattering toward the nearest exits.

That gave Yancy and me free range to go up close to the action. Veida was right next to me. She quickly started talking to her ex-boyfriend to calm him down, and I went straight up to York.

"What is going on?" I started in on him.

"Look, York, man . . . so what he said something about our dad?" Yancy spoke up, trying to talk some sense into him.

"Just because you would let it go don't mean I should. I ain't as soft as you," York shot back.

I could see Yancy getting ready to show our tougher brother that he wasn't such a pushover. So I hurriedly got in between the two of them. "Okay, this is not the time or the place, guys. You two really need to get on the same page. York, come on. Let it go," I pleaded.

I knew that he wouldn't walk away so easily, but before York could say anything, I heard the other guy say, "Get out my way, Veida!" Maurice was shouting as he pushed her. He was getting louder and more determined to stay in York's face.

"You need to back off," Yancy said to the boy.

"Man, please. You can't even keep your girl; I ain't listening to you," Maurice said as he moved in even closer to York.

Then York reached down and pulled the knife out of his sock. He pressed the button to let out the very sharp blade. The shiny object was sparkling, but the glowing sight definitely wasn't pretty.

"Oh, what, I'm supposed to be scared now? Don't play with me. I'm packing."

"Oh, no! York, he's got a gun!" I panicked and then I quickly sent up a prayer. *Lord, You see what is happening here. We need You to step in right now and help us get out of this situation before anyone gets hurt. Thank You for coming to York's rescue before he gets into some real trouble. Amen.*

"Show it to me then, man," York said, trying to keep me out of the way.

"I'll show it to you if I have to," Maurice said, stepping closer.

York moved the knife from behind him and was about to throw it, and I dived between the two of them. I couldn't let him hurt someone and get locked up for good. At that moment, I didn't care what happened to me physically. I had to save York from himself. It all happened so quickly. But suddenly, I became a protector from harm.

Chapter 2

Better
Next Time

As I went down, the knife cut my arm and blood came rushing out of it. At the sight of it, Maurice, of course, turned out to be a coward after all and ran out of the room. Veida went running after him. Both my brothers panicked and rushed to help me.

"Oh, man, York! You hit Yasmin!" Yancy shouted.

"Sis, I'm sorry. What did I do?" He sounded truly apologetic. My hard brother was breaking, and he was clearly shocked.

Though my eyes were shut from the overwhelming alarm of it all, I was okay. But the two of them kept going back and forth at each other. This was not a time to argue. I wasn't dying and it wasn't helping the situation.

Then I heard Yancy say, "Uh-oh, someone's coming."

"Come on, baby girl, wake up," York said frantically.

I opened my eyes and said, "I'm fine. I'm okay. I'm all right."

Obviously feeling a little relief, York just hugged me. I couldn't remember the last time he'd shown me that he cared so deeply. It actually felt great, connecting with him like that.

"What's going on in here?" We heard the assistant principal, Dr. Walter, say as he was about to enter the room. The only thing I could think of was keeping York out of trouble. He's a tough, edgy kid, and being in trouble was not what he needed. Once a student has been labeled, it's a real problem. When administrators feel like a student is a troublemaker, it's hard for them to lose that reputation. So I had to help.

"Where's the knife? Hide the knife," I said anxiously to York.

Ignoring my direction, he said, "As long as you're all right, I don't care about me." He was checking out my gash and already applying pressure to it with his T-shirt to make the blood stop.

"Hide the knife, boy," I whispered as forcefully as I could. He needed to understand this was no game. But York seemed a little dazed.

He definitely didn't need to be expelled from school. I clearly remembered from freshman orientation that carrying weapons of any kind could lead to expulsion.

"Is that blood I see?" Dr. Walters asked as he walked over to look at York's shirt.

Yancy tried to shield his view and block Dr. Walters from coming closer to check out his suspicion. York managed to respond, "It's just a little scratch I got playing basketball, sir."

While Dr. Walters was being distracted by York, I followed Yancy's eyes and saw the knife lying on the floor. I quickly managed to get to my feet and moved over to step on it.

Squinting, he said, "All right, I want to see all three of you in my office. I need your names so I can call your parents."

Even though my brothers got into it a lot, they always had each other's backs when trouble showed up.

Yancy responded in an overly friendly voice, "Oh, sir, we're all related."

"Oh, so you're our triplets. The Peace children? I'm very familiar with your family. Your brother is still missed to this day around here," Dr. Walters said as we all took this opportunity to look sad. "It's not too often you get triplets in the mix. And, one of you is in our A.P. classes?"

"Yes, sir, that's me." Yancy spoke again respectfully.

"Well, then I can look to you to be forthright and true and give me a full explanation of what's been going on down here. Several students came to the office and said there was a fight brewing, and here I find three siblings. I want the whole story. I can count on you, son, to set the record straight. Correct?"

"Oh, yes, sir," Yancy said, again giving the right answer as he escorted Dr. Walters out of the gym room.

Yancy looked back at me and put a thumbs-up sign behind his back. I knew he would handle it, but that meant I needed to hurry and get York straight.

I took York by the collar as soon as we were alone and said, "How you not gonna grab that knife and hide it? What is wrong with you?"

"I just had to make sure you were okay first, all right?" my brother said in a little rough tone as he paced back and forth. "Seeing blood on my sister freaked me out. Mom would have killed me if I would've let anything happen to you. I don't know why you didn't just stay out the way in the first place."

"Oh, so you're trying to say that it's my fault that I got cut by your knife—something you shouldn't even have at school in the first place? You'd better be glad it wasn't a bad cut."

Ignoring my comment, he said, "Come on. Let's get to the man's office. I hope Yancy doesn't talk the man's head off."

"If he does, it will be to soften him so he'll give us the benefit of the doubt. And tuck in your shirt so he won't see that blood again," I said as I put on my sweater to cover up my arm.

By the time York and I had reached the office, my brother had the assistant principal all caught up with our family and sympathetic with all we've been going through. However, doing his duty, Dr. Walters did find it necessary to call our mom and fill her in on as much as he knew to be the whole story. But basically all we got from him was a tongue-lashing about staying out of trouble.

My mother said nothing all the way home. She was so unusually calm that when we got home, my brothers thought they could quietly go to their room. When they did, to our surprise, Dad opened the bedroom door.

Our father said, "Oh, no, we're talking about this thing right now. Your mom called me and told me what happened. I just went through your stuff, and I want to know just what you boys are up to."

"You went in my room and went through my stuff?" York said, challenging him and trying to get around my father.

"Wait a minute, boy. Just who do you think you're dealing with here?" Then Dad took his hands from behind his back and showed us two more knives and a gun. "I figured these belong to you, York. What's this all about? And there'd better not be any bullets in here, boy."

York frowned and said, "There aren't. I don't have no ammo."

Mom had been silent so far. I knew that she was probably

thinking that it was best if Dad handled this situation. Finally, she spoke up, sounding very discouraged. "York, I just don't understand this, son. As hard as I work, as much as your dad has been through, and you don't get that all we need you to do is behave yourself?"

York said, "Sorry, Mom, I'll get rid of 'em. Shucks, we were in the office because a dude came at me. Okay? I'm not a punk. Of all the things you've taught me, Dad, you should know I got a rep."

"Please, boy," Dad said. "No excuses."

Before he could finish, Yancy cut in and surprisingly tried to help York. "He's not telling you the whole story, Dad; he was defending your honor. Pops, people were calling you all kinds of names. And even though I overlooked it, it's hard for me to hear them dog out our father. Actually, I'm sort of glad York shut the punk up. He was spreading rumors about you and that ain't cool."

It was Dad's turn to talk. "Words can't ever hurt me. It took me to be incarcerated to learn that people take hard punches with words. They try to get at you, they try to rattle you, but they're only trying to get under your skin. Somehow they think you've got it going on in some way that they wish they had. You got to learn that the bigger man doesn't get affected by what someone says.

"You boys have to understand that fighting with weapons is not the thing to do. That'll get you in more trouble than it's worth. York, having weapons this way shows that you're not mature enough to handle them responsibly. These things don't make you a man. You are a young man with too much potential to wind up spending time in jail. I'm gonna get rid of this stuff right now and don't ever let me find out that you are keeping anything like this in your possession again. And, believe me, I will be checking up on you. Do you understand?"

My brothers didn't say anything. All that York could do was nod his head and show Dad respect, knowing deep in his heart that Dad was right. And I was soaking in the fact that we had two parents in our house for the first time in a long while, and together they were addressing tough issues with us. That was an amazing feeling.

Mom was attending to the cut on my arm with peroxide. But what stirred my soul, what made me really happy, was that we were one. Things that attacked us weren't going to break us. As a family, we were united.

⟨◈⟩

"I just can't learn this, y'all. Quit trying to make me," I said to my three girls the next week before tryouts.

Perlicia got in front of me and said, "All you got to do if you mess up at all is just move a little more. I told you that."

To demonstrate for me, she shimmied to the left and then to the right. Asia joined in. Veida then got in sync with them as well. Everything in me knew that I couldn't keep up.

Asia said, "Quit being so stressed out. I'm a little nervous too. I really want this, but all we can do is leave it in God's hands, right?"

I nodded, knowing that God could do anything but fail. But I also had to do my part. I had to be confident. And more than just believing I could do it, I actually *had* to do it. To make the team you needed skills, which I thought I lacked. I really didn't even want to go out there and try. But, even so, over the last six days I had been rehearsing and re-rehearsing the numbers. When I performed the routine for York and Yancy, Yancy couldn't even look at me without cracking up.

York flat out told me, "You're a hot mess, sis. That kind of dancing just ain't your thing. You're stiff and you look like an awkward runway model. You got to loosen up and let go."

All I kept hearing was Perlicia and York saying loosen up and let go. Was that even possible? Could I even do that?

Veida pulled me over to the side and said, "Look, girl, don't you know how fun it's gonna be if all four of us make this team? I've never had best girlfriends like this. Raven and that Shay girl, they think they got something on us. There are only five slots. We're gonna break up their little happy group because all four of us are gonna make it. You can do this."

But it wasn't long before we were already broken up. We were assigned numbers and had to try out in groups of four. And none of the four of us went together. I looked good when I did it with them and I felt confident. But that was when I thought that we were gonna be able to choose our own groups. It was scary when I found out that was not the case.

Before it was my turn to go out, Raven came over and said in my ear, "Your brother carries around a knife. You got a better chance in making it into his gang than you do making it onto this dance team. Your girls are good but Shay and I are the best. You already took Myrek away from me, but that's just temporary."

At that moment, I thought about what my dad said. She was just trying to get under my skin. I already had enough of my own insecurity going for myself. I didn't need to let her add to it by taking in all she was saying. But I'm sure my dad didn't mean to retaliate with more words by throwing anyone off their game, but I just couldn't resist the temptation.

So I said, "If you were a cheerleader, homecoming queen, Miss

America, Miss USA, and Miss Universe, Myrek still wouldn't want your uptight, stuck-up self. You might need to check yourself because you will always freeze. You might be sure of yourself, but you really have no game."

The next thing I knew, the dance instructor called my name and I walked to the front. When the music started, I surprised myself—I was doing it! I had it going on. I remembered all the moves and I felt sharp. When the next song came on, I took it up a notch because my confidence was up and I was hitting the moves. I did my kicks, my leaps, and my jumps high in the air. I was the bomb. When the last song came on, I just kept talking to myself. *You can do this. You can hold it together. You can make this squad.* When it was my time to go once more, I did it.

My girls had already gone, so when I came off they were standing in the corner jumping up and down. I was pretty sure I was gonna make the squad. I looked across the room at Raven and she looked nervous. I wasn't trying to play an intimidation game with her. This was her moment, her time to try.

I had put it out there. So I walked away with my friends. We went into the locker room and squealed at the top of our voices like the teenagers we were. We were proud of each other, and we were gonna have a place on the team. Our confidence was high.

Everyone was sitting around in their little groups, waiting for the five names to be posted. When the coach came out and tacked the list up on the bulletin board, Perlicia was the first to check it out. Moments later she started yelling, "Come on, y'all, our names are there! Come on, yeah!"

The three of us stood up and hugged each other. It felt great to know our names were there. Veida joined Perlicia and started squealing too.

Asia said, "Come on. They said our names are there, let's go and look."

Just as we got to the door, Raven came over to break the news to me. "Five names are there, but yours isn't."

That was a serious blow to the gut. Was she serious?

Just then the basketball players were coming out of their try-outs. Both of my brothers were elated to see their names along with Myrek's up on the wall. I saw them jumping up and down and cheering from across the gym. Myrek looked over and headed our way.

Raven stepped in front of me and said to him, "You're gonna be playing basketball and I'm gonna be dancing and cheering for my baby. Let's go ahead and get back together now. I'll forgive the fact that you thought that girl had it going on way better than me. Everybody knows that being a Trojanette is what it's all about."

After hearing that, I just ran past the two of them. I didn't make the squad. This was so hard. In my heart I wanted it. But at the same time I was so excited for Perlicia, Asia, and Veida. They worked so hard and deserved it. And I'm not saying Raven and Shay didn't; I mean, they were good too, but I wanted to be on the team.

Myrek caught up with me and said, "Look, what are you frown-ing for?"

"She just told you. I didn't make it. She's right. You'd get more stats if you have a girl like that." I pointed in Raven's direction.

"I don't need any stats. Plus, I already have a lot because you're my girl. Do you know how many guys came up to me last week telling me how cute you are and how much they wished they were in my shoes? I'm sorry you didn't get something you wanted. But if it means anything, you still have me. And I think you should have tried out for the basketball team anyway."

I made an ugly face. "Most basketball players aren't sassy and cute."

"You can be. Quit trying to fit in with all these other girls anyway. If they're your friends, they're gonna be your friends and just like they're cheering for me, they're gonna cheer for you. Be a star. Get a real scholarship to college."

Then he walked away, leaving me to think about all he said. It was like another punch in the gut—a serious reality check. Now what was I gonna do with that information?

⟨◊⟩

When Mom pulled up at the school, both my brothers were talking their heads off. I hadn't seen either of them so excited in a long time. Since one of them was considered a nerd and the other one was practically a thug, they didn't hang out much together. But now they had sports in common. They were teammates. Of course, they had played on the courtyard with their homies for years, but the older they got that didn't happen too often anymore.

This was going to be different; this would be organized ball. It wouldn't be like when they used to watch our older brother play and could only hope to follow in his footsteps. Now they weren't going to just stand by dreaming and watching their boy Myrek as he played. They weren't even going to be on separate levels with one of them playing and the other watching with me in the stands. They both made it.

As bad as I felt for myself, there was no way I was going to take that joy away from York and Yancy. I was their biggest cheerleader. To show my support, I just started doing all kinds of grooves to the music that was playing on Mom's weak car radio.

With all of the excitement that I could gather, I screamed, "They made it, Mom! You don't understand what a big deal this is. This is so exciting!"

"I'm excited too. Your dad is supposed to be at the house. He wants to hear all about how the tryouts went," she told us. I was slowly trying to let the air out of my balloon.

My brothers were going on and on too; they didn't even realize that they weren't letting me talk. Or maybe, self-consciously, they didn't want me to have to tell Mom that I didn't make it. She was a smart lady. I knew that she'd figured it out already because I wasn't bragging on myself. She didn't ask; she didn't rub it in. She didn't make me give her all the details about how I felt when I didn't see my name up there.

She just said, "I'm proud of all three of you guys for giving it your all."

When we got to the house, my brothers kept Mom in the car and I went inside by myself. I knew they were telling her every detail. Now that I wasn't around her, she was able to really let loose and celebrate with her boys. I could only imagine all the things they were saying.

As strong as I tried to be and as happy as I was for my brothers, the tears were already streaming down my face, just knowing that my dad would be there to greet me. Before I got to the door, the water was coming so fast it felt like I was in a hot sauna turned up way too high. He opened his arms and I just fell into them.

"Baby girl, what's wrong?" he asked.

I sobbed. "I let you down, Daddy, I didn't make the team."

"You didn't let me down, baby. That was something you wanted for yourself. I know you gave your best effort. We don't get everything we want. I missed so many years not being with you guys. I'm here now and I'm proud to see you working so hard. That's what matters to me."

"But you said it yourself, Dad, that was because you made bad choices. I practiced as hard as I could. I went over the steps in my mind. I told myself I could do it. I thought I did great. I really thought my name was gonna be up there and that was only a joke because it wasn't. I was basically the laughingstock, the only one out of my crew that didn't make it."

He just let me vent. He just let me cry, while he just stroked my back. That was so comforting. He was softly patting me and telling me it was okay. And it was okay—just being there with him. Hearing him tell me that he was still proud of me really meant something.

Before Mom and my brothers came into the house, I went into the bathroom so that I wouldn't spoil their party. I could hear Dad play-wrestling with both of his sons. He was really proud that they both made the team. Then all of a sudden there was a knock on the bathroom door.

"I'm okay; you just celebrate. I'm okay," I said in a fake voice.

"It's your mom and I know you, shared a bedroom with you for years. I know that voice is not one that's okay, Yasmin. Please open the door, baby."

I opened it and quickly turned my back to her. She was an emotional person and a really good mom. She'd done so much to take care of us all by herself for so long. I knew that she would lose it if she saw me upset about this.

"Turn to me, baby," she said as her voice started to crack.

"I can't, Mom, because you're upset too."

"Baby, I'm not upset because I wish you would've made the team," she said as she stepped in front of me. "I'm hurt because my sweet girl gave her whole heart and it didn't work out. I'm your mother; of course I'd be bummed when you're disappointed. That doesn't mean we can't get through this. That doesn't mean this setback isn't gonna make you stronger. Baby, as my child, you should know with the hard times you've lived through that we don't always get everything we want."

I just hugged her tight. Yes, my dad had given me the pats, but my mom was giving me the back-and-forth teddy-bear hug. Her version of comfort was just as soothing to me.

"This girl rubbed it in my face. My girls made it. I know it's petty but, Mom, they're gonna have such cute uniforms. Then Myrek tells me that he didn't think I should've been trying out in the first place."

"He said that?" Mom said, shocked.

"Yeah, he said that he thought I should be trying out for the girls' basketball team."

Mom's voice showed that she was pleased. "Wow, he said that?"

"Yeah, but I mean, York and Yancy have always laughed at girl basketball players."

"You know they're idiots sometimes. You and I have talked about how you dunk on them all the time and shut them up real quick."

"It doesn't matter. I've already missed the opportunity to try out for the team anyway. Tryouts were going on at the same time everything else was happening."

"So then you have a whole year to get your grades up. I went online at work and was able to check your grades. So far you've got four As, a B, and one C."

"Algebra's killing me, Mom."

"You're gonna get it. I've e-mailed your teacher and he said you can come in some mornings for extra help. But now you've got enough time to stay on track and decide if you want to work toward dance or basketball. You might just want to continue modeling, or maybe you want to be the president of the United States. Whatever it is, sweetie, you can do it. Don't beat yourself up. Just know how this defeat feels and take the lesson of that girl who made you feel bad because she made it and rubbed it in your face. You'll remember that if you ever make something and someone else doesn't, you should never rub it in their face.

"Be thankful you've got . . . as much as I hate to say this . . . a boyfriend who cares about who you are and doesn't want you to be just another girl in the crowd. Your brothers, who have been unhappy with themselves for so long, finally found something that they like. Your father is out of jail; he's getting on my nerves, but at least he's out of jail. What I'm saying is, you've got a lot to be grateful for."

Of course, she made me laugh at that. She held my hand and stared at me. I could tell whatever she was about to say was coming from her heart.

"I guess what I'm saying is, we get knocked down a lot in life, but it's how you get up. It's how you give the bad stuff to the Lord that makes you better. Sometimes it's like you're in a maze and you're frustrated because you can't find the finish line. Just regroup, shake it all off, and get ready to win at your game. I always remind myself of this, no matter how bad it gets, and it just motivates me to do better next time."

Chapter 3

Happier
Days Ahead

"No, Dad, I'm not trying to do that with you," York said, as he laughed at my father.

"Oh, what's up, son? You don't want to hang with your old dad? I'm just saying, it's the weekend and, I promise you, you'll have enough time to do your homework. I just thought we'd hang out and do a little man-to-man bonding. That's all."

Mom and I were coming out of the bathroom when we overheard their conversation. She looked at my dad in a crazy way. "This is the first time I'm hearing about some road trip."

"I'm sorry. I just came up with the idea. I wasn't scheming and plotting, Yvette. I just think that maybe it's time," Dad explained.

He couldn't see York's face, but York was looking at our mother as if to say, *Please say that I can't go so that Dad will get off my back. That would be cool with me.* But Mom did no such thing. Instead, she nodded and smiled at our dad.

Then she surprised us all by saying, "I actually think it's a great idea. York needs to spend time with you. Yeah. Go ahead, son."

"Sorry, Dad, I got a game, you know? Next time though, Pops," York said, as he hit him on the back. Then he darted around me and Mom to escape to his room.

When York was in the bedroom with the door closed, Yancy came out of the kitchen and went up to Dad and said, "You ain't asked me that."

My father coughed a little nervously. "I didn't ask you because I guess I just assumed you wouldn't want to go truck driving. You're my son that's gonna be a doctor one day. So don't use that broken English."

"You think I can be a doctor?" Yancy said to him with amazement that he had Dad's respect.

"I'm not saying York can't be. I'm just saying, yeah, I believe right now with everything you've shown your mom and me, how hard you work in school, and how easy those books come to you—I truly believe you can be a doctor one day, son."

"Well, I believe hanging with you would be the bomb. I kind of always figured that you thought I didn't need you. I even convinced myself that I didn't need that whole father-figure thing. But there's been a lot of studies about young men growing up without a father and the effects it has on their life. Well, you're here for us now. So, if it's all right, I'd love to hang out with you."

Those words made Dad sink onto the couch. He put his head in his large hands and sobbed. I could tell by the loud music coming from the boys' room that York was oblivious to what was going on. But to see Dad so moved that one of his sons said he needed him meant the world to him.

"It's gonna be okay." Mom went over to comfort him. "This is good."

"Yeah, yeah, I'm all right. I know I'm supposed to be tough. I'm fine. I'm the man. I'm cool. It's just . . . I'm happy, that's all." He wiped the tears from his eyes, looked at my mother, and said, "You've done good with our kids."

"I let one get away," she said with her voice cracking. She was becoming equally emotional.

"But he's in the best hands he can be in, Yvette. Now the only thing you and I can do is try to be even better with these three we got. I'm here for you and I want to raise them with you. And thanks . . . just thanks for all you've done."

"Okay, so can I get packed or what, Mom?" Yancy asked. Clearly he was not into the gushy moment. "Can I go? I know you're gonna tell me I can go, you just told York he could go. Just because he didn't want to go is no reason not to let me . . . "

Cutting him off, Mom said, "Okay, Yancy. Go get packed. Jeffery, this is an overnight trip, right?"

"Yeah, but we'll be back early tomorrow. I won't keep the boy long. If he needs to study he can take his books."

"Well, let me fix you something to eat before y'all get on the road." Mom walked toward the kitchen with Dad right on her heels.

"I've never turned down no meal," he said to her.

The two of them went in the kitchen and she started whipping up something. I walked past my brothers' room and I heard the two of them going at it. So I stood at the door and listened.

"What you mean, you going with Dad?" York asked.

"He's taking me on a trip." Yancy's voice escalated.

"Well, he just asked to take me."

"But you told him you couldn't go."

York laughed. "So what, he's just gonna take you in my place?"

"What you mean, in 'your place'? He's my dad too. He only didn't ask me because he thought I was busy."

"Oh. So, what . . . he thought I ain't have anything to do so that's why he just asked me?"

"Wait, man, why you trippin'? I want to hang out with Dad; you don't. You told him you didn't want to go; I do. Lay off me, man. Quit acting like a girl, all jealous and stuff. You and Dad have been tight for years and now he finally wants to hang out with me," Yancy explained.

"Correction. He doesn't want to hang out with you. He's just taking you because I told him that I didn't want to go."

As he laid some clothes on his bed, Yancy unloaded on our brother. "Call it whatever you want. I do want to go. I do need a dad. I've been a knucklehead thinking he didn't care about me, mad at him because of what he did in his life that kept him from us, and now God's giving me back some time with my dad. I'm in high school. I've got a few years before I'm out of here for good. And just because you don't want to hang out with him, just because you think you're too hard-core to be with your dad, doesn't mean I feel that way."

"I got more scars than you ever will have," York said, defending himself.

"You're just a real little punk, following around with Bone in the streets like he's some big player. I've tried that road, tried to be hard, but what I need is my dad. So hate on me, I'm out." On his way out of the room, Yancy pushed past me and said, "Quit being nosy."

I didn't know what to say to that because I was being nosy. York was coming behind him, but I blocked him in the doorway. This was crazy and I had to say something.

I asked, "What's going on? Why are you tripping? You told Dad you didn't want to go. I heard it."

York said, "Yeah, but . . . I mean, it's like . . . whatever . . . forget it. You won't even understand."

I responded, "Yancy's right. You're jealous. You don't want him to have time with Dad. He's not just your father, you know?"

"I never kept him away from you. You're still his baby girl; what's the big deal? You wouldn't understand because you're the only girl in this house, but wait until him and Ma start hooking back up. And the way he's coming around here, I know it's just a matter of time before that happens. When you get put on the back burner, see how you like it."

I said to him, "First of all, Ma's not giving him the time of day, but if they were to get back together, that would be a great thing for all of us. She'd cut us all a little bit more slack, we'd all have a little bit more freedom, it might be fun. Okay? And second, if we're a tight family like that, I could never be jealous of anybody. Dad's got enough love in his heart for all of us; quit being so hot under the collar about it."

Then we heard Mom's voice. "Y'all come on out and say goodbye to your dad and brother."

York pushed me into the hall. He went back into the room and slammed the door. Why did my family have such issues?

⊰❦⊱

Mom was only working one job now, but she was definitely putting in overtime whenever she could. It was Saturday so it was just York and me. I was really getting sick of him blasting that loud music. He knew if Mom was home he wouldn't have it blaring over the top like it was. I needed some earplugs.

When I couldn't take it any longer, I went and banged on his door. "Open up, York. That music is too loud."

Finally, he opened the door, but the music was still blaring. "What is the problem? You ain't Ma; why do you want me to turn my music down? You're getting on my nerves . . . whining too much, Yasmin. Lay off me."

"Well, you're pouting too much, York. You should have told Daddy you would go on the trip with him if it was this big of a deal."

York huffed and swatted his hand at me. "I ain't even thinking about that."

"You haven't even come out of your room to get anything to eat. You're upset about something. I know you. What, you don't have any plans? You're gonna be stuck in the house all weekend," I teased him.

"I got plans. If Dad doesn't want to hang out with me, I got somebody who's gonna show me the ropes. You're tryin' to say I'm some new jack punk, that I ain't got scars like Dad, whatever. Me and Bone are about to get in the street. I'm gonna be his wing dog. I'm gonna show everybody around here who runs stuff on the high school level. Yancy can have Dad. He's an old playa anyway," York said as he turned off the music, stood up, and stared me down. I could read the bad attitude all over his face. He was saying, *What you gon' do about it, then?*

"Wait a minute. You can't leave this house, and you certainly can't go and hang out with Bone. Those days are long gone. You've already gotten into too much trouble because of him. You said you were gonna straighten up. You told Ma you would. And Dad warned you too." I tried to persuade him.

"Girl, please, don't be so naïve. You know we say what we gotta say. And if you tell them . . . ," he warned, grabbing my throat and really scaring me, "you'll get way more than this."

York went back into his room and slammed the door. All I could do was go in my room, slam the door, and lock it. Then I kneeled by the side of my bed and started praying.

"Lord," I said, "my brother is seriously tripping. If he's not selling guns, he's carrying a knife. If he doesn't cut me, he's grabbing me by my throat. What's going on with him? I mean, is he on something? Do I need to go through his room and find out what's up? Why do I always have to be the one who notices things? Something is not right with this nut. York is so angry all the time. Finally, things are coming together for us and he, of all people, needs to let some of that tension go."

Before I could even say amen, I heard the front door slam shut. "Okay, so now what am I supposed to do?" I looked up to the ceiling with that question on my heart.

It just didn't feel good. I was sitting there doing nothing, knowing that York was headed to be with Bone. He could get himself into way more trouble than he could ever imagine would be facing him. I got up, ran out of the apartment, and jogged down the street. But I didn't see York anywhere.

I did catch up with Jada, who was jogging too. As I looked anxiously around, she asked me, "Who are you looking for?"

"I'm trying to find York."

"Girl, he jetted."

Panicking, I said, "What? You saw him? Which way did he go? I got to find him."

"He's with Bone. He just swooped him up and they took off in Bone's loaded ride."

"Are you serious?" I said. "Please tell me which way they went. You think you could borrow your dad's car and take me to find them?"

"Okay," she said, "Yasmin, I know you tryin' to take care of your brother, but . . ."

"But . . . I've lost one already. Okay?" I cut her off, reminding her.

"You ain't got to tell me. Jeff was my boyfriend and I ask myself every day why did things have to turn out so bad? Why wasn't I thinking straight? How could I hurt him more than I helped him? I wish he was here."

"Well, York is here. Okay, Jada? I've got to do something."

She stopped in her tracks and tugged on my shirt, which made me stop too. "Listen, I know you want to help him. I know you want to find him, but I know Bone too, and he's nothing to mess with. He pulled up and stopped me before your brother got in his car. I know they were up to no good."

"Then that's all the more reason I got to find York. He can't get himself involved with all that."

"He's already involved, Yasmin, that's what I'm trying to tell you. Once you get caught up with Bone like that, there is no getting out. There's no getting away until Bone is ready to cut ties."

"But my dad's back and he can be crazy. He might hurt Bone for real. I can't just do nothing to stop that from happening."

"When I was Bone's girl I saw some things, Yasmin, that no teenage girl should ever see. So read between the lines. Trust me; I know Bone is not scared of your pops."

"So, what's gonna happen to my brother?"

"The only thing you can do now is pray for him."

"But I did. That's what made me feel like I needed to come out here and find him."

"Well, then God led you straight to me so that I can put some sense into you. You go messing with Bone, he'll come after you."

"What do you mean?" I questioned her.

"Well, there's only one reason he hasn't insisted that you be his girl. York is trying to be in his good graces so he'll leave the rest of your family alone."

"And if we lose York to the streets or he ends up dead or in jail, then how am I supposed to take that?"

"I'm still trying to find answers to all that myself, Yasmin. To be honest with you, not only did I lose Jeff—somebody I really did love and that I now accept I pushed away—but I also lost my baby. Yeah, I can see the baby every now and then because she lives with your uncle. But a big part of me is gone. Sometimes you just got to be smart, face reality, and handle what you can control.

"Your pushing Bone to leave your brother alone isn't realistic. And I don't even know if getting your father and mother involved is something that's smart either. I just want you to think about what you're doing. Don't go off with your first emotion because emotions can get you into trouble. Trust me, I know. Keep praying and letting the Lord lead you. I know He won't steer you wrong, and I also know that Bone ain't trying to hear nothing about what God wants. That's why I say talk to God."

I knew she was right. We walked back to my place, and she kept filling me in on just how awful Bone's street involvement was. My brother had gotten involved with a real villain, and I knew I was going to help him somehow. I just didn't know how. All I had to do was keep giving it to God. He'd help me find a way—His way.

⁂

"Ooh, girl, are you okay?" Veida rushed up to me and asked. It was first thing Monday morning and I was back at school after not making the team.

Before I could respond, Perlicia was on one side and Asia was on the other. I knew all three of them were ready to see what I was thinking. Feeling bad personally but trying hard to keep it in wasn't easy.

"We've been calling you. You won't call nobody back," Asia said, as she gave me a friendly shove.

"I started to come over there and make sure my girl was straight," Perlicia said. "I'm sort of mad I'm on the team. We got the schedule and we're gonna be practicing after school every day. You ought to be happy you don't have to be there."

The three of them forced a laugh. I knew they were just doing it to make me feel better, but I really was excited that they were on the team. Honestly, I wasn't trying to take anything away from them or make them feel like they couldn't be excited about all that was going on for them. But I had to admit, it really did warm my heart that they cared so much for me. They had called me a ton of times over the weekend. I just wasn't ready to talk about how bummed out I was. That's why when I saw their phone numbers I just didn't pick up the phone.

Asia noticed the sadness in my eyes, so she leaned in and said, "I was praying that you'd be okay. I really wished that you would have made the team and not me. You've been through so much."

It was time to head into school, but I just hugged her. I didn't care about being vulnerable. I actually had to stop and hug all three of them. I really care about my girls, so I said, "Hey, I've been through a lot, Asia, but so have you. With all that stuff happening with your stepdad, you deserve to have some joy. And, Veida, with all the problems your parents are going through and still you were there for me when I was modeling. I just want to say, now it's your turn. It's time for me to support all of you."

"What about me?" Perlicia said, slightly joking. "You want my spot because I'm serious about these practices."

I smiled and said, "Girl, you're gonna keep everybody straight. They need you on the dance team."

Perlicia nodded. "Yeah, they do. If Raven and that Shay girl think they're gonna run the squad, they've got another think coming."

Then she just kept on talking. The three of them walked away smiling and happy. I was happy for them. And that's what friendship is about. Surprisingly, getting all warm and fuzzy about their success actually made me feel better about me. It was good to discover that I had unselfish love in my heart.

⋙◈⋘

We had physical education together later in the day. Our school was all abuzz about the new P.E. teacher who was supposedly really handsome. I didn't think he was going to be all that. For one thing, I had a boyfriend. My thoughts were on Myrek, and I even tried to keep those feelings in check, not letting my mind run away all crazy with thoughts of him either.

However, when that coach walked through the door, I could not hold back my grin. The girls around me got really excited, oohing and ahhing and stuff. He was built, you could tell he worked out; he was really buff—not skin and bones like most of the boys in our school. Though he wasn't our age, he was very young. He was probably in his mid-twenties. There was no ring on his finger, and all of the girls were looking even though we were too young. No doubt he would lose his job if he talked to any of us. But as I looked around at the dreamy faces, I didn't think anything was wrong with admiring the man.

The coach called us together and said, "All right, young ladies, I'm Coach Hicks. Your coach is on maternity leave and most likely I'll be with you until Christmas break. Just to let you know, I'm also going to be the track coach in the spring. I know you all are ladies, but I believe in sports and exercise for everyone. And when girls show the guys that they're just as tough, it's good competition. So let's get to it."

We started by choosing basketball teams. That happens to be my element because I played with Myrek and my siblings since we were young kids. So I know how to handle the ball. But most of the girls were trying not to mess up their hair. They didn't want to break a sweat and get too smelly. That didn't matter to me since we had lockers and soap and stuff. Some girls were so girly that they didn't want to break a nail. I wasn't worried about that either so I just dominated. It was like playing with elementary school girls.

When coach dismissed us to the lockers he said, "Ms. Peace, may I see you for a second?"

I was actually a little nervous. Had I made a fool of myself by playing too aggressive? I didn't know him so I couldn't read into his strong face. I held my head down and waited for him to speak.

Coach Hicks said, "I just want to tell you that was a good practice. You gave a wholehearted effort out there. How fast do you run the forty?"

I responded, "My brothers say I do it in a six-five, but I think it's more like a six-two."

"Wow, are you serious?" he said as his eyes widened. "Well, like I said, I'll be coaching track in the spring and I just know that you'd be an asset."

Squinting my face, I said, "I don't know about track."

"Well, if you don't like the sprints, we've got distance running."

"Distance? No, sir."

"We've also got relay races, hurdles, and long jumps. I really want you to think about it. You could run circles around most of the girls in here. There are lots of college scholarships out there for females in track. I just want you to keep all your options open. If you get on college scouts' rosters in the ninth grade and you continue to be good, they'll follow you. Then, if you work with me, I can't begin to tell you how many offers you'll have by the eleventh grade, definitely by the twelfth."

"Did you run track in college?" I asked, wondering where his passion for it came from.

"Yes, I went to the University of Arkansas. They have one of the best track programs out there. I also competed in the last Olympics. I'm a sprinter and I push my athletes. But I only come after talent that I know is really good. You've got something special. Think about it," Coach Hicks said, as he pointed me toward the locker room to go and get ready for my next class.

When I walked away from him, my three girlfriends were huddled together, making more oohs and ahhs. I was smiling, but it wasn't because Coach Hicks thought I was cool or cute; he thought I was an asset. And after all the dejection I had faced lately, it felt great to know that this Olympic coach had eyes for my talent. Now it seemed like I could look forward to happier days ahead.

Chapter 4

Encourager
Shines Through

Sooo ... I heard the new gym teacher likes my girl," Myrek said to me at lunch. The two of us were eating our hamburgers and talking.

"I don't even know who you've been listening to. Who told you that?" I smacked my lips and responded.

"I just need to know if I need to go and beat him up. People couldn't wait to get out of class to come up to me and tell me I had competition and stuff. He's supposed to be one of the assistant coaches on our basketball team. And we were fired up about his track background, but now I'm not so sure I'm all for him. Shoot, maybe we have enough coaches." Myrek was certainly sounding a little jealous.

"Oh, stop it," I said, as I took my fist and punched him in the shoulder.

"Seriously, though. What was his interest in you? He had you stay longer after class. I mean, I hear you. I'm sure it was all legit, but what did he want?"

"He wants me to run track this spring."

"Seriously?" Myrek immediately got fired up, as if it was the best idea he'd heard ever. "You know you got speed. You challenge me all the time. When are we gonna race again? I haven't forgot that you left me in the dust when we were in the seventh grade."

Reacting to that idea, I said, "And I don't want to race you anymore because I know you're much faster now." We both laughed and finished our lunch. "I don't know . . . sports, women . . . do they really mix?" I asked.

Myrek laid it all out. "You never asked that question before. You were the first one out on the court with me and your brothers. For years, you were my biggest competition. Now you got issues with a girl and a ball, or a girl and some cleats? What's up with that? What's not to like about a girl out there doing her thing?"

"I don't know. I've changed, I guess."

I looked down at my clothes; I was dressing more hip these days. I had good fashion sense, and now I was into my girly side. I held out my hands; my nails weren't extremely long, but they were trim and neatly polished. I really liked taking care of them. Then I looked at the cute boy in front of me. A lot of girls wanted to talk to him, but Myrek was my guy now. He liked me because I had spunk, because I held his interest. I even think that he likes me to use my brain. But, would he really feel that way if I acted like a tomboy?

"You think I wouldn't like you, huh?" he said, as though he had read my mind. "I don't know when you're gonna get this. I like you for you, and I like the fact that you're not just a typical, prissy girl who thinks she's too good to break a nail. You don't mind getting your hands dirty and, because of that, you're able to school me on my own game. Besides, it was pure torture when I talked to Raven. She didn't even know what a bounce pass is."

"Really?" I asked. I wanted to make sure he really felt what he was saying.

"Yes, I want more than just a cute face."

Shaking my head and feeling unsure, I said, "I wanna believe you."

"Would you just accept what I say?" Myrek asked, as he huffed in frustration. "You're stubborn like your mom."

"What did you say?"

I was just about to take in everything Myrek was saying and not stress out so much. I really do think that sports are okay for girls, but then he had to go and say that I was stubborn. Who'd he been talking to, and why did he think he could say that to me and get away with it? I gave him a look that made him want to take back that statement.

"I'm sorry, I'm sorry. I'm just saying—"

I interrupted him. "No, I don't understand. You need to elaborate a little bit more. You can't just say you're sorry like I'm supposed to know what that means. What do you mean, I'm stubborn like my mom?"

"My dad says—"

"Oooh, so that's where this is coming from," I said to him, as I got even more irritated. You and your dad have been talking about me and my mom?"

"Well, we're guys. We hang like that. We talk about stuff and he's just thinking that maybe he can get to know your mom a little bit more if we talk about both of you. I think our relationship can be stronger too if I understand you more. So we exchange information a little bit. Is that so wrong?"

"It's wrong when you label us and say we're stubborn like that's a bad thing. You just said you like my spunk, my strength, and my stamina. Now you're sitting there holding it against me. Which way is it, Myrek? Do you want me to be some bimbo without a thought of my own, or do you want me to have my own opinions?" I was beginning to feel annoyed.

"We don't have any issues like our parents do. It's just that my dad wants to take it to the next level, and he's just really, really frustrated because your mom keeps putting him off. He's a good man. Why is she trippin'? Would she rather be with an ex-con?"

Getting up from my seat, I was seeing red. I said, "Okay. See, now you're really offending me because that *ex-con* you're talking about is my father!"

"I know he is and I'm not trying to dog him out; I'm just saying he's not as cool a guy as my father is."

"That's your opinion. Your dad is struggling with three jobs. My dad is bringing in the bank right now, legitimately, with the truck driving thing," I said defiantly.

"Isn't that a temp job?"

"So what, Myrek?" I was about to leave when I noticed him bury his head in his hands, so I sat back down. "Look, don't get me wrong, your dad has been cool to me and my brothers and even Jeff when he was here. I don't have any ill words toward your father. But can I say that he loves us as much as our own father does? No way. Would I not be happy to see my own parents get back together? Come on, Myrek."

"Oh, so that's what you want? You want your folks to get back together? You made me think you were down for our parents hooking up."

"Now that my dad is around, I guess I've changed. Your dad is still great in my book too. But I'm just saying it's not my decision to make. And I'm not all up in my parents' business, or my mom's, for sure. I wouldn't try to push her either way."

"Well, let's just agree to disagree then. In my book there is no choice," Myrek concluded.

"Fine," I said, as I grabbed my tray and looked around for my crew so I could sit with them for the last few minutes before lunch ended.

It was stupid of me to want to be with Myrek during lunchtime anyway. My girls had gotten on me, telling me that I was putting them down by trying to hang with my little boyfriend. And where was that getting me? Lunchtime with him had now given me an upset stomach. He needed to rethink how he talked to me. But, beyond that, actions definitely speak louder than words. No more.

⊸❧⊷

A few weeks later, it was the middle of the semester. We had just gotten progress reports. I had truly been working hard trying to make sure I got excellent grades in all of my classes. And my grades had mainly been As and Bs since school had started. With some extra help, I had even managed to bring up that C in Algebra to a B. It had taken some doing, but I made it. I must say that it was very satisfying when I found out that I was on the honor roll. I mean, it wasn't that I expected it to be any different. However, just to see it in print gave me a feeling that was so good. I couldn't wait to get home and show my mom. And it was Friday, so my dad was supposed to come over for dinner. I knew he'd be proud of his baby girl too.

When my brothers got on the bus with me, they both had bad attitudes. Myrek came and plopped down beside me. He and I weren't fussing anymore. He kept on apologizing and I knew my heart was supposed to hold grace. So to avoid having another argument over this, we decided we wouldn't talk about our folks anymore. If we were gonna have a relationship, we had to keep our thoughts about them out of it.

Knowing how close Myrek was to my siblings, I asked him, "What's wrong with York and Yancy?"

"We had P.E. fourth period and everybody had to show our basketball coach their grades."

"And so? What's the big deal?"

Myrek looked the other way like he didn't want to tell it all.

"Yancy's in honor classes," I said. "So, what's he got? One B?"

"Try three Cs, two Bs, and one A," Myrek whispered.

I was shocked! I had a better report card than the whiz in my family? No wonder Yancy wasn't smiling. I can't even remember the last time he pulled down a C. And, granted, he was taking advanced classes, but he always knew how to master tougher subjects and still come out with high marks. When I glanced over at him, Yancy appeared as if steam was shooting from his ears.

Myrek leaned over and said, "He's talking about dropping the honor classes."

"My mom won't even let him do that."

"I don't know, that's what he said."

"And what about York? What's going on with him?"

"He didn't even show nobody his report card, but I saw Coach getting on him something bad. I think he might be failing."

"What? Failing classes?" I questioned. But Myrek looked away again like he wasn't gonna tell me anything else. "Okay, see you are a trip." I pressed him.

"I'm just saying I don't know for sure. I don't wanna lie on your brother or nothing, you know? I do know he can't practice all next week because he's gotta go to mandatory tutoring. We were given the rules at the beginning of the year and for that to be your fate, you have to be failing. If it continues and his report card has the same grades, then he'll get kicked off the team. If he flunks both semesters, of course, he'll have to repeat the ninth grade. I'm just saying." I could tell Myrek wasn't thrilled about spilling the story, and I gave him a mean look for that.

Guys were really funny. They've got this code with one another and always want to have each other's back. My only problem with that is they should use their influence to help each other achieve greatness. Sometimes you just need to call someone out or tell on them if it would help them get back on track. But that wasn't Myrek's way of looking at it. He was basically telling me, *Don't use nothing I told you because I don't want it coming back on me.*

I didn't know what I was gonna do. I had to hold his confidence, but I had to grill my brothers too. Had they made it to high school and lost their minds? I couldn't help but wonder why I was the only one doing better.

Thirty minutes later we were at home, and the spaghetti sauce my mom had made, along with the Italian sausage mixed with hamburger meat, had the house smelling like Italy. I just knew it was gonna be delicious. But my brothers came in and went straight back to their room. They didn't even ask when dinner would be ready. Neither did they show their progress reports and own up to the fact that they weren't that good. Nothing.

I didn't know what I was supposed to do. I loved both of my brothers, but I finally made the honor roll. My first progress report in high school proved I was doing the right thing. Was I not supposed to comment on my grades just so that I wouldn't put them on the spot? I wasn't deliberately trying to reveal that they weren't meeting expectations. While I was reflecting on it all, Mom read my face.

"What you stressin' about? Let me see that progress report," she said in her most commanding voice.

How'd she know? I wondered. Yet I was inwardly relieved because now I could show her without seeming like I was trying to make myself look good when my brothers were going to look bad. I went over to my notebook to pull it out, and I thought, *You know what? When my brothers made the basketball team and I didn't make dance, they got in that car with Mom and were able to be excited about their success.* Why was I feeling like I couldn't be excited about mine? Would I be taking something away from them if I showed my parents that I had worked hard? I don't think so.

I reached into my binder and was so happy to say, "Look! Three As, three Bs, boo-yah! But, Mom, how'd you know we got them?"

"Because I've already talked to some of your brothers' teachers. They called me very concerned about Yancy's Cs that are almost Ds, and your brother York is on probation and on the verge of failing. Your dad will be here in just a few minutes and we're gonna talk about all of this."

"I don't understand," I reacted. "Why do *we* have to talk about it? I'm showing you my report card. I got good grades."

"And I'm proud of you, honey. We're having a family discussion when your dad gets here. Last time I checked you were part of the family."

Naturally, I was so mad. I wanted Mom to see me pouting so she'd cave in and change her mind. However, she didn't.

It took Dad fifteen minutes to arrive at our house. We all sat around the kitchen table and had to hear them lecture about grades and how important they are. It really got to me because I should have been exempt from that conversation. I had great news for them, but they were punishing me because of the boys.

After about ten minutes, it finally seemed as if Dad felt my pain. He said to my brothers, "You two are now in high school and you're starting to feel your britches a little bit. I don't want you to get too beside yourselves. Yancy, you can do better and we're keeping you in those A.P. classes because we have high expectations. You can do it and you're gonna do it.

"York, you got the rest of this semester to turn these Fs into passing grades. You don't need to be so prideful that you can't ask for help and get it. I know it hasn't been easy for you guys. That's why I'm not gonna punish you at this point. We're gonna give you a little more time to get it together. So much has happened in the last year and a half, but look at your sister. She's persevered through it. She's doing what she needs to do. And you can do it too. There's no reason you both shouldn't want better for yourselves, and I hope this talk will make you rethink your direction. If not, we have a serious problem and you both will have to answer to me."

꧁꧂

It was Sunday and it had been a long weekend of studying for all three of us. Because my brothers needed to get back on track and because I wanted to stay on track, we were in church. We'd officially joined almost a year ago and while we'd been going off and on, we hadn't been as consistent as we needed to.

However, since Uncle John had been here, he and his wife and the kids had been very active in our church. So much so that the pastor had my uncle going through a special program, and we were there as witnesses to him being sworn in as a church deacon, along with five other distinguished men.

The pastor said to us, "God loves us all. The church is a place where He wants us to praise His name and to uplift each other— to keep the body of Christ strong. In addition to the head of the church, we need other members to be leaders. As a second layer of support, the deacons of the church are to be armor-bearers."

Then he looked at the candidates. "You six gentlemen have gone through a journey that will enable you to assist the ministerial staff, encourage the meek, teach our youth, and just be an overall example."

I was watching Uncle John and he was smiling from ear to ear. I already owed him so much for being more than an uncle when our dad wasn't with us. I knew he was a man of God. Though he and his wife could not personally have any children, they were raising my deceased brother's child as well as taking in my neighbor's two children. The Lord had to be working in his heart to raise other people's kids like his own. They were such a precious family.

I loved that my uncle was willing to help people and serve them as if he was serving God. He made me think that, though I was a teen, I was supposed to do more too. Whatever I thought my part was in life, I am supposed to want to do better, and want to make others stronger. So, as he took the deacon oath, I also took a personal pledge with the Lord that I would try to be even better, love even harder, and be a walking example of Jesus Christ. In order to do that, I need to get in the Word more.

I had to admit, sometimes understanding much of the Bible is difficult to do. Many times I would shut the Book and move on to something else. But if my uncle could go through training, then maybe getting into Sunday school—a place where I could learn the Word and enjoy it—was definitely what I needed to do to stay strong.

There were so many things that I didn't have the answers to in my life. Particularly, like why my brothers tripped when we were right on the verge of making things great for our family. But even though I didn't have all the answers, I knew the One who did, so I had to stay connected with God. That is the way I will be able to keep reaching back and helping to pull up those that I love, those that need me, and those that God wants me to care about.

Use me, Lord. I was praying and watching with pride as my uncle went back to his seat. *Like You plan to use my uncle John, use me.* And just like my dad didn't punish my brothers but said something positive to get them on the right track, I was excited to realize I too had that gift. In order to be Christlike you have to let people know you appreciate them. Even when people you care about get down, when God is in your heart you can help them back up. You will be a better person when the Encourager shines through.

Chapter 5

Never
Stay Down

*W*hat in the world are you doing by my locker?" I said to Raven when I noticed her fidgeting with my things in the locker room.

"I was just shutting the door. It flew open. You need to buy a lock."

She was right. I did need to get a lock. It was on the supply list at the beginning of school, but I had to wait on Mom. Although she wasn't scraping pennies anymore, my mother still wasn't able to buy every single thing that the three of us needed all at one time. However, I wasn't the only one without a lock, so I didn't think it was any big deal. Still, finding somebody kneeling down by my stuff made me a little uneasy.

"I don't trust her," Perlicia said in my ear. It seemed like she had been reading my thoughts.

"What? What y'all looking at us for?" Shay said. As usual, she had her girl's back.

We all just ignored her. I wanted so desperately to ask my three girlfriends how Trojanette practice was going, but they hadn't been talking about it around me. I knew it was because they didn't want to make me feel like an outsider. Besides that, I didn't want to make it seem like I was feeling left out. So, I just didn't know how to bring it up.

It had to be pretty interesting being on a team with Raven and Shay. Obviously, the five of them had not formed any kind of freshman bond. I was secretly happy about that. I knew it wasn't right because you should always want your friends to have other friends and enjoy every part of life. But I didn't know if I'd be able to take it if my girls got along with those two.

Coach Hicks had worked us so hard. We didn't even have time to play around. We had to get dressed in a hurry or be late to our next class. The bell was about to ring so all of us quickly got dressed and rushed out into the hall. Raven and Shay were following close behind us, like they wanted to hear what we were talking about and stuff.

Veida got fed up, turned to them, and said, "Now, don't y'all have classes the other way?"

"You can't tell us which way to walk. We can walk where we wanna walk. You don't own these halls," Shay rolled her eyes and said to my friend.

"Just come on." I grabbed Veida's hand and we hurried on to get to class. But as usual, we slowed down to pass through the tenth grade hall. Being freshmen, we had to be careful and cool. So, we had our little strut down. Then we started to hear more and more giggles from the crowd forming behind us. That definitely wasn't the reaction we were going for.

Finally, Perlicia couldn't take it any longer as the laughs got even louder. She said, "What is up with you all? Why is everybody laughing?"

She went over to a tenth-grader from her neighborhood, and the guy whispered something in her ear. Immediately, she came up to me and pulled me over to the side.

"You gotta go to the bathroom. Now!"

Confused, I asked, "Why? What's the problem?"

She looked behind me and said, "What? You forgot to bring a pad this morning or something?"

"I don't understand what you're talking about," I said to her, getting frustrated.

Squinting her eyes, she said, "You don't feel weird, wet, or anything?"

"Spit it out, girl. I don't get what you're saying."

Perlicia called Veida and Asia over and pointed to my back. Together, they made a shield behind me.

Getting angry, I said, "Why are y'all covering me up like this? What's going on?"

"You need to get to the bathroom now!" Perlicia insisted, yanking me across the hall into the girls' restroom.

"You got one?" Asia said to Veida, still evasive to me.

"Naw, my time was last week," Veida responded.

Then it dawned on me what they were referring to. "Oh, don't worry. I'm not coming on until next week sometime."

"Well, that explains it," Perlicia said, leaning in to me again. "It came early. Didn't your mama tell you to always have a spare?"

"Y'all are trippin'. I don't feel anything. I'd know if I had started, thank you."

Simultaneously, the three of them turned me around to the mirror. I looked behind me and couldn't believe there was a big red spot on the back of my pants. I rushed into the stall in shock.

I quickly prayed. *Okay, Lord, I know my body. Nothing is happening right now, so what's wrong with me? This is so embarrassing. Everybody's laughing at me. Please show me what to do.*

As I was slipping off my pants, I immediately smelled ketchup. Suddenly, it dawned on me. Raven and Shay played an awful prank! I went back out of the stall and explained to my friends what had happened. "So this is what they were doing at my locker!" Naturally, this was a serious problem for me.

"Okay, see . . . it's on now!" Perlicia said.

"That's just stupid. They need to get a life," Veida said.

Felling really sad, I asked, "What am I gonna do? I don't have no other pants, and if I wash these I won't be able to dry them. It'll still look like I had an accident."

Asia said, "Go back down to the gym."

"Yeah. Our dance teacher, Ms. Smith, has a whole closet full of extra clothes because people always leave stuff," Veida explained.

"I don't wanna just wear anybody's stuff."

"She washes it all for emergencies. And don't sweat it because when we see Raven and Shay, we got this," Perlicia said as she took her hand and made a fist.

Veida gave me her sweater and I tied it around my waist. When we came out of the bathroom, there was a small crowd waiting to get a look at the ninth-grader who didn't have her life under control. I tried to look strong, but Raven wanted to humiliate me and she had been successful.

Ten minutes later, I was bawling in Ms. Smith's office. I couldn't hold back the emotion any longer. "First of all, I hate that I didn't make the dance team. Raven did. So I don't understand why she had to do this to me."

Ms. Smith was listening to me and writing a report. She asked, "When you saw her at your locker, what did she say? I just want to get clarity because I'm reporting this. I don't want her thinking that this is funny or acceptable."

"No, no. Just let it go," I said, wanting to forget this whole awful ordeal.

"I'm not going to let it go, Yasmin. I will talk with her and she will be reprimanded. Let's see if she thinks missing the first few games of basketball season is funny. She won't be making these stupid pranks anymore. Trust me on that one. But listen, you've got to stay tough. Out of sixty girls, you were the sixth choice. It's just that I only had five spots. I want you to stay out of trouble—no fights or anything like that. Keep your grades up and keep on practicing your dance moves. I believe you can be on my squad next year. Unfortunately, some girls get a little too full of themselves when they make the Trojanette team."

Ms. Smith helped me find some cute pants, and I actually looked better than before. Talking about it had really helped me to work out my frustrations. She gave me a pass to class and reported the incident. I just prayed God would give me a heart to forgive Raven and let it go.

The week flew by. I knew from Raven's bitter look at me every time we passed each other in the hall that she didn't like the fact that she couldn't perform at the first four basketball games. It wasn't my fault; it was because of her own silly behavior.

Basically, she was just jealous that Myrek was still my boyfriend and not hers. He and I had an understanding. As long as Myrek didn't give Raven any reason to think she could challenge me for him—then he and I were straight.

Myrek's birthday party was Saturday, and my girls were spending Friday night with me so that we could all go together. York and Yancy were going with us and afterward they were heading over to Dad's for the weekend. We weren't sure when his temporary job would end, but it was the reason he was allowed to live in Jacksonville. One thing for sure, we knew it wasn't going to last forever.

My mom was helping Mr. Mike with the party. With the streamers and balloons scattered throughout, their apartment looked pretty festive.

"Can you go and pick up the cake?" Mr. Mike asked my mom. "I already ordered it and paid for it. I just forgot to pick it up."

She responded, "Yeah. Everything looks great here. The kids should be arriving soon. I'll get the cake. No problem."

"Thanks," he said, as he leaned over and gave her a kiss on the cheek.

Perlicia, Asia, and Veida all gave me a weird look. Seeing them have a grown-up moment felt kind of weird to me too. I was dating the son; Mom was dating the father. Yuck.

Then Myrek asked me to dance. I had no problem at all with that. We hit the floor. Yancy went up to Asia and they started dancing while York pulled Perlicia out on the floor. Veida was left sitting alone and I could tell she didn't like it.

After the first song ended, I said to Myrek, "I'ma hang out with my girl for a minute."

"Yeah, Veida's got the long face. Don't let her stay upset. It's my birthday."

"I know. Don't worry, we're gonna have a good time." I went over and sat beside Veida. "Okay, so what's wrong?"

"I'm the odd man out."

"What do you mean?"

"Well, I mean, I know what I want. But I know what I did too. And it doesn't seem like Yancy's ever gonna forgive me. I understand why, but I really still like him. Why'd I have to act like I was interested in both of them, knowing all the time I really liked Yancy?"

I just put my arm around her. I knew that I couldn't control my brothers. Part of me wanted to stop trying because every time I put my nose in their business they just pushed back on me. When I looked over at the door and saw Raven and Shay standing there, I realized I needed to pay attention to my own business.

Veida noticed them too and commented, "Okay, so why'd Myrek invite them?"

We got our answer when we watched Raven and Shay go up to Myrek with a big box they had brought. He was smiling way too wide, all too happy to take the present wrapped with Christmas paper in October.

"Where's the happy birthday paper?" Perlicia came over and said. "Hey, Veida, I'm sorry. I wasn't gonna dance with him, but Yancy just pulled me out there."

"It's okay, it's okay," she said. "Better you than some girl who wants to get with him. You know what I'm sayin'?"

We all nodded since we knew how trifling girls could be. Myrek was starting to look around. I had a feeling he wanted to talk to me, but he was blocked by Raven who was pulling on him. It only took a minute before she had him out there dancing.

By the time they were on song number three, the party was crowded. I just kept watching Myrek. Yes, it was his birthday and we were supposed to mix and mingle and have a great time, but it wasn't like he was looking for me any longer. He was all too into being "Mr. Popular." Maybe having a girlfriend was cramping his style. I wasn't amused by watching the show Raven was putting on so I went outside. Just then my mom was pulling up.

She yelled out, "Where you think you going? I need to keep an eye on you, honey. What's wrong, Yasmin? Talk to me."

I walked over to her car. "I don't know where to start, Mom. It's Myrek. I don't think he needs me to be his girlfriend anymore."

"You don't think he *wants* you or *needs* you? Because those are two different things."

"Really? It feels like it doesn't matter. It feels like it's the same thing. I'm wrong for him and I need for us to break up."

"Okay, so why are you saying this? Because it's his birthday party and he's having a good time and Miss Yasmin ain't the only person here he wants to have fun with? It's a party, sweetheart. Don't be one of those girls who tries to keep a guy from being himself. Myrek is a nice-looking young man. He's also a good guy. He's got a lot going for himself. Of course other girls are going to think that's appealing, and of course other guys are going think he's cool and want to hang out with him. Right now he still thinks you're cool, and although your dad doesn't want any part of y'all dating in the first place, I'm trying to be realistic. I think if I keep an eye on you two and not try to keep you away from each other then y'all will make smart choices.

"But, honey, what you're saying will drive any good guy away. A needy, clingy, young lady who pouts all the time is very unattractive. Snap out of it! Be the Yasmin I know he's fond of. The one who's spunky, independent, strong-willed, and confident."

Mom had it all figured out and she was right. I helped her carry in the cake and she had helped me straighten out my attitude. It was my guy's birthday. So I decided to give him some space. After all, why couldn't I let him enjoy his special day without feeling bad because he wasn't spending all the time with me? Yeah. I'm glad I had a mom who could keep it real. Keep me in check.

We took the cake to Mr. Mike who was in the kitchen. His face frowned up as he saw the vanilla frosted single-layer cake. Mom shrugged her shoulders. I was confused.

"Wait, this isn't what I asked for. I ordered a chocolate cake. He doesn't like butter cake," Mr. Mike said, as he read the label on the side.

"I guess you took too long. The people said that cake was gone. They didn't have another chocolate one, and I knew all these kids were here for a party so I got the best cake that I could. What? It's not my fault you forgot to get the cake."

"Yeah, but what other kind of cake did they have there? I wish you would have called me before you just made a decision."

I kind of felt uncomfortable and sort of in the middle. At the beginning of the summer, she and Mr. Mike had gone out a lot. But now that my dad was back, things had tapered off a little bit.

It wasn't that Mom was going out with Dad instead. But I don't think Mr. Mike liked the fact that he was forced to be around my father so much. Clearly, the tension between them had mounted.

"What's going on?" Myrek came into the kitchen and asked. "The cake looks good. You guys ready to eat? Thanks, Ms. Yvette."

"Obviously, it's not the right kind, so I'm sorry." My mom looked away, letting it be known that her feelings had been hurt.

"No, no it's fine," Myrek said, looking at his dad.

"What, son? Why you looking at me like that? What? You mad at me because I'm saying it's the wrong cake? I ordered something else."

My mom cut in. "I understand that and I'm sorry it's not what you wanted. I was just trying to do you a favor. Besides, the credit card you gave the lady to pay for the cake didn't go through either. Maybe that's why they gave the one you ordered to someone else. So I paid for it."

Mr. Mike's voice got louder. "What? You want your money back? Is that what you're saying?"

"Dad, all my friends are here," Myrek said, trying to calm his father down.

"Yeah, Mom! Quit arguing!" I was trying also because I knew both Myrek and I were very embarrassed.

Then, who did I see when I turned around? None other than Miss Raven smiling from ear to ear. I just wanted to bop her.

"It looks like you got this under control," Mom said to Mr. Mike. "I'm out."

As she headed for the door, Myrek's dad was close behind her. The apartment didn't have enough windows for all the nosy teens trying to be in grown folks' business. I'm glad our parents knew not to make it an even uglier scene. But I could tell when my mom didn't come back inside that whatever she had with Mr. Mike was over.

"Girl, you think it's gonna be good for us to still spend the night with you?" Perlicia asked.

My friends really were my friends. We were so connected. Our thoughts were so much alike.

"She didn't say y'all couldn't come. Besides, she knows your parents aren't coming to pick y'all up tonight, so I think it'll be all right."

"We'll just stay out of the way because I know she's gonna be crying and all that other stuff tonight," Asia said. "When my mom broke up with that guy after all he had done to me, I heard her wailing in the house for weeks."

When we sang happy birthday to Myrek, I actually felt bad. His dad looked really bummed. It wasn't my business to say he was making an issue where none was there. But aren't relationships supposed to be a good thing, a healthy thing, a fun thing? When it couldn't be that anymore, then two people needed to go their own ways and move on.

After what just happened, how was I gonna help my mom not be sad? I didn't want to rush Myrek's party, but I was happy when it was over because I wanted to make sure she was okay.

Then, to make matters worse, my father showed up. I was frozen in my tracks when I saw how upset Mr. Mike was when my father stood at the doorway. He had come to pick up my brothers.

"Hey, pumpkin," my dad said when he saw me.

When he hugged me, I moved him out of the small living room as quickly as I could. He didn't know it, but I knew he wasn't invited. We certainly didn't need another adult drama.

"What? You embarrassed to hug your dad?"

I didn't want to tell him all that had been going on with Mom. I didn't know what to say, but I had to say something. Otherwise, my face would give it away.

So I uttered, "It's just not a good time, Dad. Okay?"

"You ain't in here cuddled up with a boy, are you? I thought that Myrek and I had an understanding. My baby girl is not ready to date. I told your mama too."

"No, Dad, it has nothing to do with that. I'll tell York and Yancy to come on out."

"What's going on, Yasmin? Why are you trying to get rid of me?"

After asking him again to just wait outside, I walked back inside to get the boys.

"Yeah, you do that," he responded. "I certainly don't want to get that Mr. Mike upset anymore than I'm sure he is, losing a great lady like your mom. But you know, sometimes things aren't supposed to work—"

"Dad!"

"I'm just saying," he commented, as he threw his hands in the air.

Then Perlicia whispered to Asia, "As cute as her dad is, I can see why her mom broke it off with Mr. Mike."

Asia agreed. "Yeah, he must have been lifting weights in jail. He's buff!"

When I heard that, I turned around and gave them such a mean look.

I was relieved when ten minutes later, Dad and my brothers

were gone. But I didn't want to leave until Raven's parents came and picked her up. Leaving her with Myrek after all that was going on—uh-uh, I wasn't crazy.

About an hour later Myrek told me, "Hey, it's getting late and I'ma help my dad clean up. Why don't you and your friends go on to your place. Y'all helped us set up. He's not happy right now and I just need to deal with him."

"But, Raven?"

"Come on, you know me. We talked about this. I mean, what is she gonna do? Give me another Christmas gift? You're my boo," Myrek said, as he kissed me on the forehead.

When I opened my door, I was actually surprised not to hear crying when we walked inside. My three girlfriends went straight to my room and turned on some music. I guess they wanted the party to continue. But I was worried about my mother so I went and knocked on her door. "Come in," she responded. When I opened the door she was reading her Bible. I could see a big smile on her face.

"I don't understand," I said.

"What do you mean, baby?"

"I mean, you just broke up with Mr. Mike. He's all mad at the world and you're calm, cool, and stuff."

With a smile she responded, "Well, everything in life is not gonna work out, Yasmin, but you can't fall apart when it happens. When you have a heavy heart, you got to give it to God. Let Him lighten your load. I am disappointed that things didn't work out with me and Mike, but that's in God's hands. I know He's going to allow us to still be friends. It might take a minute for even that to happen, but when God is the center of your joy—you never stay down."

Chapter 6

Braver
and Stronger

On Saturday afternoon when my friends were gone, I noticed my mom's long face. I knew she had put up a brave front with me, making me think she was okay with things being over between her and Mr. Mike. But I was never a naïve girl. Now, even wiser as a teen, I knew she cared about him. And if it was over, that had to hurt. Maybe it just took a few hours for her to realize it. Whatever the case, if she needed me, I was going to be there.

I realize that I wasn't her peer and she tried to shield me from things that she didn't want me worrying about, but still we were tight. We'd shared a room for years. She was more than just my mom; she was my friend, and I couldn't let her go through something without me going through it with her. Just recently when I was sad because I didn't make the Trojanette dance team, she was there for me.

So I offered, "Mom, you want me to fix you some hot tea or something?"

"Oh, no, sweetie. I'm okay." She was sitting on the couch, pretending to brush away some invisible crumbs.

I sat beside her, rubbed her shoulder, and said, "Mom, please talk to me. You're usually strong, but you're sitting here and it's obvious that you're sad. You told me everything was okay, but clearly it's not okay. Open up. I'm here and I can handle it."

I hated that she thought I was still her baby girl. I knew in her eyes I'd always be that kid, but she had forgotten about the times when she would talk to her friends on the phone and I'd be right there. Then she wouldn't care that I heard everything. Why the change now?

Seeing I was so worried and wanting her to talk to me, she leaned forward and took my hand. "Yas, I wish life was perfect. I wish I could always be strong, particularly for you. You're my daughter and I know life as a black female can be hard. And it's particularly difficult when you make bad choices. For me, I've got to carry that burden in my gut—wishing, wanting, and hoping I can make things better for my family. But that's why I tell you to think before you act. You can't go back and undo past mistakes."

As she kept talking, I realized this was more than just about Mr. Mike. She was in a deep funk, and I hadn't seen her that way since Jeff's death. I didn't know if I'd ever told her that it wasn't her fault that he was gone. I knew that she thought it was and she felt responsible. However, she needed to know what I thought.

I squeezed her hand as she looked out our window and took in the view of our dismal neighborhood. I said, "Mom, you know there's a lot of stuff I found out that was going on with Jeff that we didn't know before. It's really none of our fault, especially not yours. He wasn't doing well in school. He thought Jada was having somebody else's baby, and people from around the way were asking him to throw the championship game. Mom, he had a lot of pressure on him that had nothing to do with us."

She stroked my cheek and said, "Thank you, sweetie. I needed to hear that. But it's so much . . . and even though I might look sad, trust me, I'm okay. It's just sometimes we just need to step back, reflect on past mistakes, and go to God so He can make us stronger from them."

"That's what you were doing? Praying?"

She let go of our grip and motioned for me to move closer. "Yeah, I was having some quiet time because there's something I want to teach you. See, you may not always make the best decisions, but it doesn't mean you can't learn from your mistakes. And when you go through things in your life and it hurts, you can grow from them. Truth be told, I hate that I didn't know everything that was going on with my son. I don't question why I was working two jobs, trying to put food on the table. I know it was because I never got a college education. And I didn't have help because the person who I was supposed to depend on made bad choices and ended up incarcerated. I think both your dad and I learned from that. We have three children left here and we want to do the best by you guys."

"Mom, we're okay."

"Yeah." She looked out the window again. "But my sons need their father."

"So, knowing that they're hanging out with him more makes you feel good, but makes you feel bad too?" I asked.

"Something like that, baby. Something like that."

"I'm glad that he's around now, Mom."

"I know you are, baby. How's your arm doing?" She saw me rubbing it.

"It's better. I've been putting that stuff you gave me on it."

"Well, I wanted to talk to you about that too. Yasmin, you can't get in the middle of other people's drama. I know you care about your brothers a lot, but you guys are in high school now and they're gonna have to make their own choices. Jumping in the middle of a fight wasn't the smart thing to do."

"I know, Mom, I just couldn't see York get expelled from school for good."

"Good thing you didn't need any stitches. I tell you, York has such a hot head. He hasn't learned how to control himself. He just needs to sit still sometimes."

"What do you mean, Mom?"

"He came in here earlier this morning and asked me if I had fifty dollars. He said that he needed it badly but wouldn't tell me what he needed it for. I told him I needed fifty dollars too, and before I knew it he was gone. He thinks everything is supposed to come easy. But life is just not that way."

"Where is Yancy?" I asked her.

"He's still hanging out with your dad."

"That's good they're bonding."

"Yeah, I guess I just have to let my boys go. They don't need me as much anymore."

"They need you, Mom."

We just hugged. I was happy to know that she was human and when things bother her, she knows how to take them to God. I was taking a lesson from her struggle.

My old digital clock read 12:42 a.m. when I was awakened by loud voices outside my window. At first I thought I was dreaming. But the voices only got louder. I sat up, rubbed my eyes, and started felling uneasy when I heard the startling conversation.

"I don't want you comin' with me, boy," I heard Bone say to York. I moved my blinds and saw him with my brother pinned up against his car.

"Come on, Bone. Come on now. I need to work off the money I owe you," York pleaded.

Bone let him go. "Why you ain't say that in the first place? Your sales have been down and I don't want the loot back; I want the dough."

Wow, Bone still had York selling something. Probably the weapons he was always hiding. I was happy his sales were down. Kids didn't need that. But Bone wasn't letting York off the hook. This was a really bad thing either way.

"I'm headed up to Atlanta. I ain't going on no picnic. Are you down if it gets dangerous?" Bone asked my brother.

York nodded. I wanted to scream out, "No, you can't handle it!" But remembering what my mom told me, I thought before I reacted and said something stupid. I said nothing.

Bone continued. "This dude up there took off with my money and I don't play that. I need to get my cash. Taking you might work. Don't nobody know you. You can go up to the door for me, and then me and my boys can take care of business. They'll never know what hit 'em."

York was fired up. "I'm down, Bone. Come on, I'm down."

"All right, all right, little homie. You're in. It's 12 something now. We should be back tomorrow before dark. When we get back, the two hundred dollars you owe me will be erased. I might even break you off an extra hundred with Christmas coming in a couple months and all."

"Then, what you waitin' for? Let's go." York opened up the car door and hopped inside.

All of a sudden my heart started racing. Two hundred dollars sounded like a lot of money to owe somebody. Was York crazy? Was he really gonna ride with Bone? Were they gonna beat up somebody, or worse? What was my brother thinking? That was crazy! Quickly, I put on my sweat suit and tennis shoes. I knew Mom had also just told me that I shouldn't get in the middle of everything going on with my brother. But I couldn't help but feel like his keeper.

Unfortunately, as soon as I got outside I saw no sign of anyone on the street. Bone's car and York was gone too. I couldn't believe this! I stomped my foot on the ground out of frustration.

Turning to the only One I knew who could help, I prayed, *Okay Lord, please protect my brother. Keep him safe. If I'm to help, what am I supposed to do?*

I ran back in the house and peeked into my mom's bedroom. She was sound asleep. Yancy was staying overnight at Dad's, so he couldn't help me think of what to do. I paced around the house. Minutes later, I went back to Mom's bedroom door. I wanted to go in and wake her and tell her all about what was going on. She could get in her car and go after Bone, but what good would that do? I heard them say they'd be back tomorrow. York would just have to tell her where he'd been. So I went back to my room and fell across my bed. Somehow, I drifted off to sleep.

At ten the next morning, I woke up to my dad and brother peering into my room. Then, before they disappeared, Dad gave me a wake-up call. "Baby girl, you gonna sleep all day? Your dad wants to spend some time with you."

Thinking that maybe everything with York was just a bad dream, I got up and dashed back to my brothers' room, only to find two beds that hadn't been slept in.

I heard voices coming from the kitchen, so I went in and said to Yancy, "You talked to York?"

"No, he left us yesterday. He didn't want to go on the second run with me and Dad. Look at the loot I got!" Yancy held up a couple of twenties.

"You weren't supposed to show your sister that," Dad jumped in. "I know I made you work for yours by riding with me to keep me awake and help unload the truck. But here, Yasmin, sweetie." Dad handed me the same amount.

"She didn't even work!" Yancy protested.

"She didn't have to. That's my baby girl. I take care of her like that."

Little did he know, if York had been there at that moment I would have given him the money. Now I realize that everything I remembered was not a dream at all.

"Jeffery, that other son of yours has been workin' my last nerve," Mom said with an attitude. "He didn't come home last night. I've been up since seven and he's still nowhere to be found."

Then my parents sat down at the kitchen table and drilled Yancy about all the possibilities of where York could be. I went back to my room and just sat on the bed. I placed both of my hands over my head and thought, *This is a lot. This is real.*

But should I say anything? York was supposed to be back later today. The last time I got in his business he got really upset with me. I had tried to stop him from getting involved with that no-good Bone. I almost thought that our relationship would be damaged forever. Now I was torn because he was gone out of the state with Bone. Didn't our parents deserve to know? But really, what could they do if they did know?

"Yancy!" I called out, trying to make up something to get him away from my folks. "Could you help me with this?"

He shouted back, "I'm talkin' to Mom and Dad."

"Boy, go on in there and help your sister," Dad said, looking out for his daughter.

As soon as Yancy got to my door, I yanked him into the room and shut the door. "I know where York is."

"Oh, well then . . . tell—" he said loudly, before I cut him off.

"Shhh!" I said, as I placed my hand over his mouth.

When I pulled my hand away, he asked, "What? What's up? What has he done now?"

"Last night, York didn't know that I heard him talkin' to Bone outside my window, but I heard it all. They were talkin' pretty loud. I can't believe Mom didn't wake up."

"He's with Bone?"

"Yeah, they went to Atlanta to get some guy who owes Bone money."

"Yancy rode with him?"

I continued. "Yeah. Bone's gonna pay him."

Yancy said with worry in his tone, "We got to tell Mom and Dad now."

"But he's supposed to be back before dark."

"How do you know that?"

"Because that's what Bone told him. They were gonna roll up there, take care of business, and come right back. It's just a few more hours from now. Why don't we ask them to take us to lunch or something? That way we could keep them out until he comes back home. We don't have to get them all worked up, right? Why should I tell them now?"

Mom was curious about what we were up to and was already on her way to check on us. Suddenly she busted in the door. "Yasmin, what's going on? What do you know?"

Yancy turned around and walked out of the room. "I guess you got your answer. You should tell because she asked."

I filled my mother in and I could see the worry all over her face. She started crying very loudly. Dad heard all the noise and came to see what was happening. He just held her and said, "He'll be all right. I know he's fine. York is tough. We'll keep believin' he's okay."

"You don't know that! Bone is really bad! Jeff got mixed up with him. York just wanted some money and I didn't have any to give him. And so now he felt like he had to get it any way that he could. Oh, dear Lord! What have I done?" she cried.

"It's not your fault," Dad said to her. "Yasmin heard them say they're supposed to be back before dark. I'm gonna stay and wait; is that okay?"

The only problem was, nine hours later we were still watching the door intensely, and York hadn't showed up yet. We were sick with worry. All four of us were about to break. Where was York?

"Mom, I'm scared. Where is he? I don't understand why he's not back. I know what I heard. They should have been back."

Yancy said, "Maybe they stopped off to eat. Or, Yas, maybe you didn't get it right."

"I really wished it had been a dream, but I know it wasn't. Bone had York pinned up against his car. I saw them from my window."

"I believe you, honey," Mom said.

I went up to her and said, "I should have woken you up right away. Mom, I'm so sorry."

I felt horrible. This was a lot. York was missing and it wasn't no joke. So many things went through my mind and none of them were good. The biggest thing that scared me was the reality of the deep level of trouble York could be in by hanging with Bone. Thinking about all the serious possibilities was overwhelming.

My parents went back to the kitchen and talked. I tried to study, but that wasn't going well. So I was glad when Uncle John came over to help them sort through everything that was going on. They called the police. However, since it hadn't actually been twenty-four hours the police wanted us to wait before we alerted them. They weren't able to officially file a missing person's report yet. Myrek came over and he and Yancy were about to take off into the neighborhood looking for York.

"Where are you guys going?" I asked them before they left.

"We got this," Myrek said. "We're together. Everything is cool."

"You need to tell Mom and Dad where you're goin', Yancy."

"I'm not goin' anywhere. I'm just steppin' around the corner, all right?" Yancy said to me, as he gave me a look that meant I needed to chill out.

I wanted to convince them not to go because the last thing I needed was for Yancy to go off and get himself into trouble too. But I had to let them do what they thought could help. After all, most of this really seemed like my fault. Although, after playing it all over again in my mind, I couldn't really think of anything else I'd do differently. Wake up my mom? What would that have done? She wouldn't have been able to find him.

However, I did need to get on my knees and pray. *Lord, I know it seems like I always need something, but I'm coming to You for my brother York again. I asked You last night to protect him and cover him, but he's not back. Only You know where he is, Lord. This is scary. But if I know he's in Your care, maybe I can help my mom not be so stressed. You know she can't lose another one of us. She's tough; I realize she's strong. But she has shown me that she's vulnerable, and I guess right now I'm vulnerable too. I mean, I'm thankful Dad is here, but this is all just so hard. We just need Your help. Please, Lord.*

An hour later, our house was like Grand Central Station. Word got around fast. People in the neighborhood were coming by and the phone kept ringing. My parents looked frustrated and Yancy and Myrek were not back. Then we heard a police siren go off as it was zooming down the street.

My mother started crying again. "Are they headed here? What's going on? Oh, dear Lord! It's my baby!" Dad rushed to her and held her close to calm her down.

Uncle John tried to help. "No need to panic until we know something."

One of our neighbors looked out the window and said, "No, they're not comin' this way. Something else must be going on . . . the car is headed to another building. Everything's okay."

What a relief that was.

A few minutes later, Myrek and Yancy were back. They both looked at each other with neither one wanting to spill the beans. They were breathing heavy and their faces looked like they were in serious pain.

"Spit it out, what's going on?" Dad said to the two of them.

"It's Bone," Yancy said, stopping and looking away.

"What does he mean, it's Bone?" Dad asked Myrek.

"Sir, some Georgia cops just made it to his mom's house. Bone's been found dead. They're on their way over here."

My mother started yelling something awful. I just fell to the floor and started crying too. Yancy was trying to hold it together and be strong for us, but he lost it and fell into our father's arms. This was horrible news. It wasn't looking good for York at all.

When the cops came, they explained that there was gang activity and that Bone's car was shot up and his body was found in his car. The sheriff said, "Ma'am, we understand that your son was supposedly with the victim; is that correct?"

"We think that they left the state together and were heading to Atlanta, sir. Please tell me my baby is okay. Do you have him in custody up there? Please tell me something good," my mom said, as she clutched at the officer's crisp uniform.

"At this time, ma'am, your son is missing."

"Oh, no! You don't even know where he is," she cried.

"Ma'am, at least at this time we can confirm he has not been a casualty to this crime. It was a pretty rough scene to view, and right now they are questioning the other young men who were at the scene with the victim. We'll get to the bottom of this."

"You gotta find our boy." Dad went up to the sheriff with tears in his eyes. "We lost a son about a year and a half ago ... and we ... we ... we—you just gotta find our boy."

The officer said, "I understand, sir. We'll do everything we can."

"I'm coming with you," Dad said, thinking that was a good idea.

"No, sir. Right now I need you to be here for your family. As soon as we have any word, we'll contact you immediately."

When the sheriff closed the door, it really seemed that York might be gone for real. How could we deal with that? How could we handle that? God had to help us. Knowing that Bone was gone, I had to let myself ponder the thought that my brother might be gone too. My folks were losing it. But I had to stay hopeful that we would get through this crisis by being braver and stronger.

Chapter 7

Freer
Hearts Abound

*I*t was the longest four hours I'd ever spent in my life from the time the police left our home until we finally got some news about York. To break some of the tension in the house, Dad and Yancy went out with Uncle John. Mom and I were together waiting. She had calmed down and mellowed somewhat from her hysterical state. When the phone rang, I knew what she was thinking: it was either good news or bad news.

I would have given anything and everything I wanted for Christmas—even the hope of ever being a Trojanette or having a famous modeling career—just to have my brother back. I love York, I know my family loves York, but because we were going through this scary situation I was able to really understand how much and how deep that love really is.

"You want me to get it, Mom?" I said when it rang for the fourth time.

"No, sweetie, I'll get the phone. It's gonna be okay."

"Yes, Mom, it's gonna be okay," I said, as I stood beside her and held her hand. We walked to the phone together and, just before it rang the fifth time, she picked it up. Her voice trembled. Her knees were shaking, but she answered it anyway. I could feel her being strong. Then I prayed quickly, *Lord, You're bringing us to it. People have said that You will also bring us through it. We've been through a lot of hard things as a family, but yet we're still here. I don't know about this phone call, but I know You're still God. Make it all right for our hearts. Make it all right for our souls. In Jesus' name, we need Your strength. Amen.*

"Hello," my mother said.

I could hear through the phone as the officer spoke. "Is this Yvette Peace?"

"Yes, it is," she responded, holding back the welled-up tears. It actually felt like I had butterflies in my stomach at that moment. The man hadn't identified himself just yet, but he sounded extremely important. My gut feeling was confirmed when he said, "My name is Carl Gates and I am the state patrol commander for the state of Georgia. I'm calling about your son, York Peace."

"Yes, sir. Do you have some news about my boy?" my mom asked.

"Ma'am, I just wanted to let you know that your son has been found and he is safe. We're questioning him now. An officer will be bringing him home shortly."

"Oh, thank You, Lord!" Mom screamed out. "My baby is all right! May I speak to him, sir? Please, may I speak to him?"

"Yes, ma'am. Please hold for a minute."

While she waited, Mom stretched her arm toward me and waved for me to come closer. I put my arms around her waist, and she and I held each other so tight. When he came to the phone, she said, "York, baby, are you all right? Let me hear your voice, honey. Talk to Mama."

"Yes, Mom, I'm all right. I'm sorry I scared you. It's just . . . some guys came . . . and Bone . . . he told me to get out of there. I just got out of there. I was scared but I didn't want to leave him like that. But then all these squad cars and stuff showed up, and I just got scared, Mom. I just ran. I should have never left home, Mom. I'm sorry, Mom, I'm really sorry."

"Baby, you just tell the police everything you know. Don't you worry about a thing. They're gonna bring you home safely. I'm glad that you learned a hard lesson. Now is not the time to talk about what went on. York, I need to tell you that I love you from the bottom of my heart."

I heard a car pull up and I ran outside. It was Dad, Uncle John, and Yancy. I shouted out, "He's okay, y'all, he's okay!"

"What?" Dad said. "How you know? How you know?"

Tears of joy came down my face. "Mom's on the phone with them now, York and the state patrolman from Georgia. They found him. He was hiding. Bone told him to run and he did. I'm glad he's okay! They're gonna bring him home after awhile."

My dad just swooped me up in his arms and swung me around in the air. The excitement in both of us was major. I looked at Yancy and my brother just smiled. He and York had a relationship like a summer day. At one point in the day there was a nice breeze and the other part of the day was blazing hot. So it was good to know that Yancy was elated to hear our brother was okay.

Uncle John just grabbed my father from behind and laid his hands on his shoulders and started praying out loud, "Lord, we thank You for taking care of York. We thank You for working out the tough stuff and for being in places where we couldn't. You're such a sovereign God and You make crooked places in our life straight. While we mourn at the loss of Bone, a young man stuck in the streets, we thank You for giving us back York. We ask You to help him realize that You've got something special for him. Lord, may we be good stewards and follow in Your Word. May we continue to love each other the way You want us to, and may we keep giving our all to You, releasing our burdens. Amen."

Uncle John, his wife and kids, Dad, Mom, Yancy, and I were waiting up when York came home. He and I didn't speak a word, but I could tell he'd been through an experience that had changed his life. He hugged us all so tight. He went on and on repeating how glad he was to be back at home.

"You just can't take nothin' for granted. Life is too sweet," he said. "I used to think being tough and hard was pulling out a gun and showing I had muscle. When Bone told me to run, I ran. He knew he was in trouble and he protected me. He showed some courage. It got real dangerous real quick, so I jetted. But I just left him there to die."

York looked away and my father went up to him and rubbed his shoulders. "You're right, son. I'm glad you can see what Bone did was true honor. That wasn't your fight and that's what your mom and I have been trying to tell you. If you keep going down this knucklehead path, you're gonna end up in a grave way before your time. I heard about all the stuff Bone had been doing: selling illegal stuff, running a crooked organization, and disrespecting the authorities. If he'd put any of those leadership skills, finance skills, or business skills to good use and not illegal things, he would have been a much better person."

"He shouldn't have had you in the car with him in the first place," my mother cut in and said in a strongly disapproving tone.

My dad waved his hand as if to say, *"All right, we all know that."* But then he said, "I understand the mentality Bone had, and I respect him for making that crucial decision when he told you to get out of there. You escaped all the turmoil that happened and you're back at home with your family who loves you. So, York, you've been given another chance, you've got an opportunity to make something of your life."

"I want to, Dad. I wanted to do it for Jeff, but now I want to do it for him and Bone."

"I know, son, that's honorable. But you also have to want to do it for yourself first."

Uncle John tried to lighten the situation and cracked a corny joke. While it wasn't really funny, we all understood that he was just trying to soften the mood so we laughed anyway. It helped a little because we were all edgy and needed to relax some. The kids were getting sleepy so he and my aunt said good-bye and left.

⋘⟐⋙

Then Dad broke some bad news that none of us needed to hear. "The temporary job I had for the last three months is over now. And based on my probation, I'm only able to stay up here in Jacksonville if I'm working. So it's time for me to head back down to Orlando. . . ."

"No, Daddy!" I said before he could even finish what he was saying.

"Yeah, Dad, I've been excited about all the time we'd been spending together. How hard would it be to try and find another job in this area?" Yancy asked.

I saw the expression on his face when York looked up at my father, like *"Please, man, don't you leave me too."*

Mom walked out of the room and went into the kitchen without saying anything. We couldn't see what happened, but the next thing we heard was a loud clatter of dishes hitting the floor like she dropped a platter or something.

Dad rushed toward the kitchen. Looking back at us, he said, "Y'all stay here, everything will be okay. Let me talk to your mother."

"Yvette, what's going on?" he said to her.

"I'm not even trying to talk about this now, Jeffery. You can go on back to your hotel, to your brother's house, back to Orlando, or wherever you need to go. Just leave me here with the kids again. Let me deal with all this by myself."

"What are you saying? Why are you being so upset?" he asked.

"Because, Jeffery, this is a lot. How do you think I'm supposed to feel? Do you think this is easy? The kids are opening up to you, even Yancy, for goodness' sake. Yasmin finally has her father around. You're helping to monitor everything that's going on in their lives. That's a good thing. I wouldn't have been able to get through this stuff with York without you being here. And now you're talking about leaving? I'm like Yancy. I mean, how hard is it to really try and look for a job right here?"

"Wait now, Yvette. The kids can hear us."

"I know that. I'm sorry. I'm frustrated and I'm upset, and I can't act like this is no big deal."

"Come here, baby," Dad started. It seemed like he wasn't sure what to say.

Before he could get any more out, Mom charged, "Are you kidding?! Get back! Don't call me baby. Just go. Get out of here. Get out of here!" she screamed again.

My dad just looked at her and grabbed his keys without even taking time to say anything to us. The three of us just looked at her like she had taken away our favorite toy or something.

The pressure was on her. "Y'all don't understand so I don't even need any attitude or lip from any of you. I've been doing this by myself for far too long. He finally steps in for a minute, and as soon as it gets a little too hot to handle he wants to step back out. If y'all want to, go live with him! And I'm sure as soon as you tell him that plan he'll come up with some other excuse to be missing in action again. Clean up this kitchen! And, York, don't you step foot out of this house. Scaring me half to death like that."

After she had let loose everything that was on her mind, Mom went into her room and slammed the door. The three of us just looked at each other. As happy as we were to make it through the night, life was getting heavy all over again. But there had to be a better way to deal with our feelings. As York stormed off to his room and Yancy picked up the broom and started sweeping, I was determined to figure out a way to actually do that.

❦

"I'm just gonna keep it real with y'all. Mom is really actin' like a spoiled little girl," York told us. The three of us were waiting for our dad to come back and pick us up. It was exactly one week later from the day when he announced that he was leaving.

Our mother was the toughest woman I knew, but I mean, she was human and she had feelings too. We all knew we were a handful. But it seemed like she couldn't make up her mind whether she wanted me and my brothers to be close to Dad or not. Just recently she had said that my brothers needed their dad. Now she'd seemed to completely change her feelings about that.

"I just think we need to help Dad find a job close to home," Yancy said. "Or maybe we can write a letter to the judge explaining that we really need our father here."

"I think he already has that kind of provision," I reminded the two of them. "That's why they're allowing him to be up here in the first place. But he still has to have employment."

Changing the subject, York asked, "How long is this modeling thing gonna last anyway?" He said it in a way that let me know he wasn't thrilled about going to my fashion show gig.

I could tell by the frown Yancy had on his face that he wasn't too excited about going to support me either.

So I just came right out with it and said, "You know what, guys? It's been all about y'all for so long. You all made the basketball team and I'm glad about that. But I mean, show me a little love too. Don't hate on me because I finally got a call for me to model. I haven't been modeling in what? The last five or six months? The lady called this week and I'm real happy about that. Before Dad leaves he wants to see me on the runway, and y'all are tripping? It's not gonna kill you to cheer your sister on for a few minutes. Is it?"

The two of them looked at each other. They knew what I was saying was the truth. I know the truth is hard to take sometimes, but I always let my brothers push me around. I stand in the background and don't really say what I'm thinking because I want to tiptoe around their feelings, their issues. But not this time.

Thinking about how much I give of my heart to make sure they're all right, I said, "So, you know what? If y'all don't want to go, stay here. I'll have Dad to myself before he heads out of town. And if the show doesn't take too long, then maybe afterward he can come back, pick y'all up, and we can go to dinner or something."

After having my say, I went into the bathroom and finished touching up my face. It was hard for me to tell my brothers what I really thought, but it did feel good. As soon as I came back out of the bathroom, I heard the doorbell ring. Knowing it was Dad, my brothers were standing by the door ready to go. They couldn't say they were sorry, but I knew that their actions said that they were.

We were going to a holiday fashion show at a department store. I hadn't been up on the runway in a long time, but just knowing that my father was out there made me relax and gain the confidence that I could nail it. I really wanted to show him my skills. The director believed in me enough to give me a call and offer me the job. That really meant a lot and I wasn't gonna let her down either.

When the show started, I was ready to strut down that runway. So when my name was called and I was queued, that's exactly what I did. And I walked proud. I did all the right moves, left foot over right, turned, pivoted, and held my head high. I was stepping to the music. I was showing off the clothes. I was accenting my style and I felt secure. It felt like a breeze.

And then I looked down at my father, a man who had been so absent from my life for so many years. He was sitting in the audience with the biggest smile on his face and, suddenly, I became emotional. It was good that I had made it back to my starting point. I only needed to hold it together for a few more seconds while I posed before exiting off the stage. Then I didn't know what to do because, as soon as I got off that stage, tears just started to flow.

How could I handle having my father being present in my life only for him to be absent again? I don't know; maybe Mom had it right. This was so unfair, and although he had apologized time and time again for leading a life that put him behind bars, we were still having to pay the consequences as a family.

When she saw that I was upset, Miss Hall went and got my dad. He came backstage and said, "What's wrong? Talk to me. You did so well, I'm so proud of you."

I just put my hands up and beat them on his chest. I felt like a little girl and I needed my dad. He needed to know that he was hurting me. So I let it all out. "Why do you have to leave? Why do you have to go? Just when we're starting to connect, just when I'm starting to see that you really care, you're gonna leave us! This isn't fair, this isn't right. Why do I have to live without a dad?"

He just held me tight until the pounding ceased. I couldn't hug him back, but I felt like a princess in his arms. I'd said some things that I wish I could immediately take back. My dad was doing the best he could to clean up the mess he had made. When I looked into his eyes, they were red and watery and full of sorrow. I realized he was hurting too, and this wasn't the way he wanted things to be. But his love for me could reach beyond the miles. This would always be a moment when I could look back and remember what it felt like to be in my daddy's arms.

My father lifted my chin and said, "Know that I'm proud of you, Yasmin. Know that I care about you and know that I am sorry. My bad choices are gonna take me away from you for a while, but I'm gonna be doing everything in my power to find work in Jacksonville."

"I'm sorry, Dad," I said to him.

"Hush, sweetie, that's okay," he said, as I laid my head on his chest again. "You can always talk to me. We can always keep our daddy-daughter connection real. Let my life and my mistakes be a lesson to you that what you do has consequences, and you got to own up to them. You've got to let people express their thoughts because the only way to go on and be strong is to live as though freer hearts abound."

Chapter 8

Tighter
Bonding Rings

*Y*ork had been down and depressed since that fatal incident with Bone. Seeing my brother who was usually upbeat and spunky barely getting out of bed and hearing him cry himself to sleep at night was way more than I could take.

When he got hurt in the fire and was in the hospital recovering, he never whined and moaned this much. I knew he cared a lot for Bone, and I could only imagine what York witnessed up there in Georgia. But to have him back and for him to be so distant now was really hard. There was talk in our neighborhood that a lot of Bone's old crew was gonna go and retaliate. As weird as York was acting, I was praying that he wasn't going to be a part of anything like that.

Lord, I prayed, *I don't really know what's going on with my brother. Well, I mean, I guess I do know what's going on. He's grieving and I feel for him because I do know how it feels. As tough as he is, I know he needs somebody. Help him to open up to us, Lord, and help him*

*lean on You. It seems like he's got it all bottled up, and I don't want him
to explode. Thanks for always being with us. Thank You for allowing me
to care about others so much. In Jesus' name. Amen.*

When I got up and went by his door, I was surprised to see
York in my mother's arms. She was holding him just like she would
cradle a baby. Mom looked up and saw me. She didn't scold me for
staring, she just smiled. I smiled back and kept on walking.

When Uncle John and Yancy came through the door, they startled me.

"Hey, Yas."

"Hey, Uncle John."

"Your mom back there?"

"Yes, sir. She's with York."

"Where have you been?" I said, looking at Yancy. He was anxiously pushing Uncle John forward like he had something important that he needed him to do.

Something was going on, something I didn't know anything
about. I could tell by the way Uncle John wasn't responding quickly
enough to Yancy's movement that he wasn't too keen on the plan
either.

"Mom, Uncle John's out here to see you!" Yancy yelled.

"I just told you she was with York."

"Her being in there with him ain't gonna make him stop cryin'.
I don't get it. That boy was tougher than Jeff and now he seems
weaker than you."

"Ha, ha, ha, that's so funny," I said to Yancy, as I went over and
popped him on his head.

"All right, you two, calm down," Uncle John said. "Don't rush
your mother, Yancy, your sister is right. She'll be out soon enough."

"I'm just saying, you got to talk to her. You got to convince her," Yancy insisted.

"Convince her of what?" I asked.

"This is man's business, girl."

"Uncle John, what is he talking about?" I said, completely ignoring the fact that my brother wanted to keep me out of the loop.

"Don't tell her anything," Yancy said to Uncle John. "You say something to her and she'll run in there and talk to Ma before we get a chance. Then Mom's mind is gonna be made up before you even say anything to her."

When Mom was coming down the hallway, her face looked so tired. It seemed like she was carrying the weight of the world on her shoulders and just needed some relief. Yancy had a point. She had been in there with York, comforting him and trying to make him know that everything would be okay. But he still wasn't ready to come out of the room.

"I don't think now is the time," Uncle John said to Yancy. He couldn't help but notice the same thing I did about her not being in a happy mood. "I mean, why pile more onto her?" he asked.

"This will take some of her frustrations away," Yancy said in a serious tone. "Uncle John, look at her. She needs a break."

Why did Yancy think that I wouldn't be for our mom needing a break? I thought to myself as I listened to the two of them go back and forth on whether or not to talk to her.

"Hey, John," Mom said, as she entered the room. She went right over to him for a hug.

"Hello, Yvette. Yancy called me early this morning to come and get him. He told me it was okay with you."

"What's this boy up to now? These kids are running me tired.

It's my day off from work and I don't feel like I got the day off at all. They work me so!"

"Well, listen, Yvette, the kids are always welcome to come over to my house."

"Yeah, I know that but you and Lucinda got your hands full right now yourself."

"Well, Yancy's got an idea. I don't know how you and Jeffery will think about it, so I'm just gonna lay it out there and you two can talk about it."

Mom looked over at Yancy as if she were thinking, *Okay, why am I hearing something from your uncle that you needed to discuss with me first? That's not how we do things in this house.* I could tell she was getting more upset by the minute. Whatever he had in mind, I hoped she would be okay with it. If it was about giving her a break, I was all for that.

I said, "It's all right, Mom."

But then Yancy gave me a look like it might not be all right. I didn't know what to think. My heart started racing.

Uncle John finally cleared it all up when he said, "Yancy thinks that it might be better if the boys went and lived with their dad."

"John, what is this? A joke or something?" Mom started questioning him as she heard what my uncle had to say.

"Okay, Yancy, you better explain this to me. And, John, don't even go looking crazy. I'm glad my son feels he can talk to you. But as far as going to live with his dad, Jeffery ain't even settled nowhere. Going to live where? Do you even know where Jeffery is? I haven't even heard from him."

I could tell Mom was really upset, and I was taken back too. Yeah, she needed a break; the three of us were a handful. But the idea of my brothers moving out to live with our dad? My feelings were hurt just by hearing this.

"See, Mom, I knew you were gonna get in the way, I knew you were gonna . . ."

"Watch your tone, boy!"

"Yeah, you don't need to speak to your mom like that," Uncle John reprimanded.

"John, you know what, you can just go ahead and leave. I need to talk to my son alone."

"Naw, Mom, I want him to stay. I knew you would just dismiss my idea. You won't hear me out. It's not that I don't love you or nothing like that, you know I do. I just want to be with my dad. I think you need some help, and I don't think you need to carry this weight and pressure all by yourself."

"Look, I'm gonna let you talk to your mom, Yancy." Uncle John was ready to bow out.

"That's fine," Yancy said to Uncle John. "Just bail. You said you were gonna be in this with me, and you were really gonna help her understand what I was feeling. But now you're backing out."

On his way out the door, Uncle John said directly to Mom, "Look, I'm sorry. I didn't mean to upset you. You are doing a great job with the kids, and I wasn't trying to undermine that or anything. I'm new at this parenting thing and I don't think I know it all or know what's best. And I certainly know you don't need me telling you what to do. So please don't be mad at me. I apologize. I wasn't trying to run anything. I just . . . I'm sorry for getting in the way."

Clearly my uncle was frustrated too. After he left, Mom looked at Yancy and said, "Okay, what's all this about? You got the man choked up, putting his nose in business where it doesn't belong. Why would you go to him because you want to spend time with your father? What, you don't think the discipline around here is good enough? You don't think I'm challenging you enough? You think the bad grades you been getting is my fault? Talk to me, Yancy. Don't sit there all tight-lipped now."

"All right, Mom. I don't know what to say for you to understand this. It doesn't really have anything to do with you other than the fact that you've been the one taking care of the three of us for so long. What's wrong with us giving you a break? What's wrong with me wanting to be a young man and be around my dad? Sometimes I do wish I was a little tougher like York, and like Dad. But I can't do that if I'm never around anyone strong like them. York's always in the streets. He's not trying to teach me nothing. Uncle John used to have that place in my life. But, I mean, he's got a family now. Dad is out and I had a ball with him when we were together."

"Yeah, I guess you did have a ball with him. That was like a honeymoon, baby," Mom said. "He was gonna get you all the ice cream and all the cake you wanted. That's not reality. He doesn't know what it's like to be a parent on an everyday basis. And, guess what? Now he's gone."

"Well, I talked to him, Mom. And if you say it's okay, I know he would want me to come down there."

"So what exactly did you say to him, Yancy, huh?"

"Yeah," I finally spoke up. "What did you and Dad talk about?" A part of me was really disappointed in our dad. Did he think that it was okay for him to raise the boys and not to raise me? After all, I need a father just like York and Yancy. Didn't he want me around too?

Yancy answered Mom. "I didn't even tell Dad nothing about this because I knew the first thing he was gonna ask was if I had talked to you. I didn't know how to talk to you, Ma, so I went to talk to Uncle John about it. And you should listen to him. He could say it in a way that you would get it. But, no, he chickens out. As soon as you told him to get out, he jetted. I got more backbone than that."

"So, stand up to me, son. Tell me what it is you want me to understand," Mom said, as she got really choked up.

She sat down on the couch and put her hands over her face. She didn't want us to see her so vulnerable, but I knew this was breaking her heart. This was tearing her up. I was hurt for her because she really thought she was losing her sons. She had just been holding one of them in her arms, and now she's listening to the other one standing right in front of her. Unfortunately, he was saying nothing she wanted to hear.

"Do you have your dad's number? Can I talk to him?" she asked.

"He was gonna talk to his parole officer and then come up here to see us. I told him about York not doing so good and he's concerned. He should be here after awhile," Yancy responded.

"So what? You thought I was just gonna let you have your stuff packed and let you go off with him?" Yancy couldn't even look at her when she started talking. "I'm not giving you up, son. I know your dad wishes he had his time back with you guys, but this is my time now and I'm not gonna let you go off and live with him. My answer is no and that's final."

Clearly she was finished with the conversation. Mom got up and went into her room, slamming the door behind her.

"I knew she wouldn't understand," Yancy said to me with a disgusted look on his face.

"I can't believe you want to leave," I said to him.

"You living here with Mom, Yas, that's cool. She's a woman. She can tell you about all that stuff."

"So you're thinking that just because Dad's a man you should be with him?"

"I don't know, but I do know that I liked being with him. I felt myself getting stronger in a way like Mom could never influence me. What's wrong with me really wanting a tighter relationship with my father? It's obvious that someone needs to get through to York. And the only one York has admired for years is Dad. He needs him too."

I said, "Well, Mom said no—so that's final."

"Dad ain't here yet." Yancy didn't think it was over yet. He was making me very aware that things could be changing.

I just dropped my head. Bonding was an important thing, but tearing a family up in the process to achieve it—maybe that was just too high a price to pay. Again I needed God to work this all out because we sure couldn't.

When Dad arrived, he and Mom reached an agreement without too much of a problem. Then Mom put on a brave face when Dad left with York and Yancy. They weren't going to live with our father, so maybe that's why tears weren't pouring down. Instead they were going to hang out with him for the weekend.

Mom was actually pretty surprised that Dad took her side and told Yancy that he was better off living with Mom. He talked about the stability that was here and the love that she had for him. He knew Yancy was getting upset as he pouted and walked away, but Dad reassured him that he cared and he loved him. He reminded Yancy that he wanted them to hang out together as much as possible.

Surprisingly, Yancy changed his attitude and was okay with everything. He realized that we weren't adults yet and that our parents did know best.

⚜

Knowing that the boys would be gone for a couple of days, I was glad to just have some girl time with Mom.

"So what are we gonna do?" I said to her. I really wanted to pull her out of the funk she was in. The recent events had really been pressing on her.

"We're gonna stay home and relax. One of the neighbors said she was gonna come over. She and I want to watch some movies on DVD. Why don't you see what one of your friends is doing?" I could tell she was trying to snap out of it.

"Do you mind if it's all three? 'Cause if I invite one of them and the other two hear about it, there's gonna be trouble."

"They're sweet girls. If their parents say it's okay, I'm fine with it. But I'm not pickin' up nobody," she quickly added.

"Thanks, Mom," I said, giving her a big hug. "And I'm glad everything worked out with Yancy."

"Yeah, I'm still a little concerned about York, and I'm glad your father got him to go along. He wasn't crazy about the idea, but at least he's out of the house. It gives me hope that when he returns things can start to get back to normal around here."

Two and a half hours later, my room went from dead silence to four teenage girls screaming at the top of their lungs over nothing. Veida's dad picked up Perlicia, and Asia had walked over. My mom and her friend Yolanda went to pick up pizza, so we had the place to ourselves. For some strange reason it felt good to just scream.

"Why are you screaming?" I said to Perlicia.

"Because, girl, I'm sick and tired of dance practice—dance practice early before school, dance practice after school. I mean, I've never been on any organized anything, and I get that we all need practice. It's just that some people need more than me because I can dance better than everybody else. Anyway, today I'm chilling and I'm here with my girls. *YEA!*"

"Asia, why are you screaming?" Perlicia asked her.

"I'm screaming because I never do anything but go to school and go to practice and come home. Yeah, we talk on the phone sometime, but most of the time we've got homework so we don't even really get to do that a lot. Having another sleepover when we just had one a couple months ago—I'm so psyched!"

"Veida, why are you screaming?" I asked her.

"My parents are back together and happy. I don't know what happened or how they worked it out, but I'm screaming because now I know what it's like not to live in a perfect world. And, to be honest, I never looked down on anybody else, but I just appreciate what I have going on. I'm just glad stuff is back on track at my house."

"And why are you screaming, girl?" Veida asked me. "Where are the boys? I'm sorta glad Yancy's not here but I'm kind of bummed too," she said, holding her head as if she was in pain.

"Why?" I asked.

"Well, my dad wasn't gonna let me spend the night if he knew Yancy was here."

We all nodded because we knew what she was talking about. Not that my mom would have allowed it anyway.

"I guess that's why I'm screaming. My brothers didn't want to live here anymore, y'all."

"What?" they said in unison.

"Well, York hadn't even been talking much since everything happened with Bone."

"Yeah, that's a lot," Asia said.

"You know some people want to retaliate against that crew up in Atlanta. I hope he's not gonna be a part of anything like that. He's quiet all the time and it's hard to know what he's thinking. I don't know what all he went through. He's so different."

"And Yancy wanted to leave you all too, Yas?"

"Yeah."

"Why?" Asia said.

"Yeah, why?" Veida repeated.

"I don't know. He just misses having a father, and now that my dad moved down to Orlando he just wants to be with him."

"So, is he gonna move?" Perlicia said.

"Umm, no. They'll be back in a couple of days. So I'm screaming because the boys aren't here!"

Later on that night after eating pizza and just sharing girl talk, we had another serious moment. We realized that we were enjoying each other's company, but we were also serious about having real true friendship. So we decided that we needed to pray for one another. That way, we could take our friendship to an even deeper level.

"I care about you guys," I said to them after we prayed. "I never really had friends like this. Thanks for coming on short notice and hanging out with me. It was hard when you guys made the dance team and I didn't make it."

"We know," Perlicia said. "But it showed us what a real friend you really are. You still cheered us on. You didn't try to steal our joy. The least we can do is be real friends with you."

Then Perlicia started to open up. "I know I don't talk to you guys much about my family."

That was so true because none of us really knew a lot about her. She and Asia were friends the longest, but Perlicia and I had drama back in middle school. Perlicia was just this real tough girl who hid her true feelings. I don't know why she seemed so angry all the time.

"I have three younger brothers who've always looked up to me. It's a lot of pressure because my parents want me to keep good grades and always act like some kind of angel. Since both of them work long hours, I have to look after my kid brothers and make sure they do their homework and eat dinner and stuff. It's even harder now because of the dance practices. I just want to be myself and not have so many responsibilities. But now I know I have friends that I can talk to. That makes it a little easier. I feel better, like I belong more. And to me, that's what makes this all so special," Perlicia said, pouring her heart out to us.

At that moment the only thing we could do was lean into a group hug. In our own way, we were a family. We were soul sisters. We care about each other and want to see each other do well. I never want to lose that feeling with my girls of tighter bonding rings.

Chapter 9

Defeater Doesn't Win

I couldn't believe my mom had agreed to let me go on my first date. Well, that was probably because Myrek and I wouldn't be alone. His dad was going to be with us the whole time. We were just going to the movies and to dinner afterward. Still, it was my first time out with a guy, and even though Myrek's dad was going to be our chaperone, I couldn't help but be excited. I felt like butterflies were fluttering in my stomach.

Of course, I wanted the night to go perfectly and so I was very nervous. I tried not to have any high expectations so I wouldn't be let down too badly, but my mind couldn't help but wonder what it was going to be like being out with a boy. Would he think my hair was pretty? Would I put my foot in my mouth by talking too much? When we ate dinner, would his dad sit at another table so he'd be able to see us but not necessarily hear us? At the movies, would he sit behind us, in the same row, or way across the theater?

I was in a daze when Mom knocked on the bathroom door.

When I opened it, she said, "All right now, Ms. Lady! You've been in there for an hour. It doesn't take you that long to get ready in the morning to go to school. And it doesn't need to take you that long to get ready to go out with Myrek. You're a beautiful girl, both inside and out. You know that. Just mind your manners and enjoy tonight."

"I don't know why, Mom, but I'm nervous."

"That just means you like him and you want to feel special. There's nothing wrong with that."

"He's gonna get you out on a date and wish he never would have known your name," York passed by and teased me. That sounded more like the York I was used to.

"Boy, get out of here!" Mom said to him. "Doesn't your sister look pretty?"

"She all right," York said. "I can't believe you're letting her wear one of your dresses."

"Of course. You know this is one of my dresses?"

"Yeah, Mom, you always look good. And, sis, she look all right too. But can I talk to her for a second, Mom?"

"Yas, I'm sure Myrek will be here in just a few minutes, so you need to come on. Don't keep him waiting, girl," Mom insisted before she left my brother and me alone.

"What, York?" I said to my brother, not really wanting to hear anything he had to say since I was sure he was going to be silly.

"Naw, I just want to talk to you seriously for a second."

"Yeah, what's up?"

"Myrek is my boy."

"I know that. We've all been friends for forever."

"Yeah, but I just want to make sure that he keeps everything on the up-and-up. You'll tell me if I need to straighten him out, right? But don't be trying to lead on him and give him mixed signals."

"His dad is going with us, for one thing. And two, you know Myrek is a perfect gentleman. And three, when did you become so overprotective?"

"I don't know. I'm sorry. I guess you're just my sister and I want to make sure no one pulls a fast one on you. Not even my best friend, if that makes any sense."

I grabbed his face and squeezed his jaws and said, "That makes a lot of sense. You care about your sister. Aww, isn't that sweet?" It was my turn to do the teasing.

"Whatever. I don't . . . ," he started. He didn't really know how to express his feelings, but it was hard for him not to show how much he cared. And that meant a lot to me.

Then the doorbell rang. I was too jittery to run and get it.

"You go get it, it's not for me," York told me.

"Go get the door, please!" I demanded.

"I'll get it!" Mom called out, hearing us bicker back and forth. It was my other silly brother, Yancy, at the front door.

He had been dropped off from studying. "It's just me," he said with a smirk.

"Boy, you have a key," I reminded him.

"Mom, tell them to leave me alone!" I protested. "They know I'm nervous. They're playing with me on purpose," I complained.

"It's just your brothers. You should know them by now. They don't mean no harm."

When the doorbell rang again, I tried hard not to be excited. But I couldn't stop the inner glow that I was sensing. I felt like I was being lifted out of the air and spun around. My first real date!

Mom answered the door and Myrek stood there with flowers. She invited him in and he walked straight over to me, handed me the flowers, and kissed me on my cheek. I knew that took a lot because, not only was Mom watching, but my brothers were standing there thinking, *Man, I know you ain't goin' down like that.* But he didn't care. He wanted to make me feel special—and he succeeded.

"You guys have a good time," Mom said, as she looked out the window and waved to Myrek's father.

Before we got to the door, Myrek stopped and looked me in my eyes, saying, "I've been wantin' to ask you out on this date for the last three years."

"No, you haven't." I tried to sound surprised.

"Yeah, I have and it's finally happening."

"I know it's gonna be awkward with your dad around. He'll probably be all in our mix, huh?"

"No, he's got a date in the car. We're really gonna have our own time."

That threw me off. Did he just say his dad had a date in the car? It had only been a month since he broke up with my mom and he already had a date. What? Who was this lady and why did I even care?

Okay, the lady was really nice, but the next three hours were a blur. Myrek's dad didn't give us any privacy. The four of us sat at the same table, and in the movie theater we sat right beside each other. In the car, the adults took over the conversation. They laughed and talked so loud that Myrek and I couldn't even hear ourselves burp.

When Myrek walked me back to my door, he said, "I apologize. I'm sorry. I had our first date planned out much better than this. All of a sudden my dad had to take somebody out too. I guess he wants to make your mom jealous or something."

"I don't understand," I admitted.

"Naw, I'm just saying. This lady came from nowhere; then out of the blue, he's all into her. I think he just wants you to go back and tell your mom."

"I guess. This wasn't what I had in mind either, but at least we got our first date out of the way. And even though I wasn't the center of the night, I felt like the center of your world."

"You were. Yasmin, thanks for going with me. Good night."

As soon as I got in, Mom hugged me and sat me down on the couch. She sounded very excited, "Okay, tell me all about it. I can't wait to hear it. The boys are back there watching some kind of scary movie. They'll be busy for a while. Come on, let's have some girl time. I got some chocolate chip cookies and milk. Don't leave out any details!"

I didn't know how to tell her because I didn't want her to cry and be upset or anything. Then she said, "Mike should have taken someone too so he wouldn't have to be all into you guys."

I just smiled at that.

"Girl, what does that look mean?" Mom sensed something was up.

"He did have a date, Ma, and I was worried you'd be upset about it. Myrek thinks his dad wanted to make you jealous."

"Jealous? Me? Ooh, Mike needs to move on with his life. You got to do things for the right reasons and, if that's true, he doesn't get it."

⚜

"Okay, so come on, come on, you can do this, Yasmin. Let's go!" the track coach said to me during tryouts. There were only going to be fifteen girls on the track team and we'd been practicing for a week. I honestly didn't care if my name wasn't going to be up there, because as hard as I worked, he was on me that much harder. I mean, I was giving him everything I had, but it seemed like he wanted more. Yeah, tough coaches might make you better in the end, but it seemed like he was being too tough. I felt like his expectations were too high and he just needed to lay off. So instead of running the last lap, I walked. As I was trying to catch my breath, all of a sudden, the coach approached me.

Coach said, "Okay, so what's this? What's this attitude I'm seeing in you? You're one of my best athletes out here. You can do the long jump incredibly well. You're a great hurdler, you can run long distance, and you can sprint. I don't understand; what's the issue?"

"I don't understand either. You told me to go out for this. You told me I have such great talent. But every time I turn around, you're on me. You're not satisfied. I don't really want to be on your team. I'm sorry," I said as I walked toward the gym.

"Oh, so you're just gonna quit because I'm on you and I'm giving you a little challenge? You're just gonna give up and not try anymore?" he challenged me.

Each step I took away from the track, I actually became more irritated with myself. Yes, it was hard and no, it wasn't fun. But I enjoy being the first to cross the finish line during practices. I find it fulfilling to have something to do at school other than just study and then go home to do chores and homework. Modeling was still my passion, but maybe track could be my sport. I have always been competitive, particularly with my brothers. So why did I find myself walking away from all of that, like it didn't matter, like I didn't care?

As I thought about it, I could hear my dad say, *"My baby girl is not a quitter. If I can endure jail, certainly you can take a rough coach."*

Then I heard my mom yelling, *"Come on, Yasmin, you can do it, girl. You got spunk, you got attitude. Use that to keep strong."*

I could even imagine York and Yancy telling me, *"You gonna punk out? Not my sister. I think you got more to give, sis. Come on."*

I had to tell myself that I had to believe so that I could achieve. So I stopped walking and turned back around to go and find the coach. But I didn't have to look far because he was still standing there. It was like he was waiting for me right where I had scampered off. "You gonna at least give it another try?" he asked. I appreciated that he was making it easy for me.

"I don't know," I said, taking a long time to respond.

It was November in Florida so it wasn't hot. The weather was getting cold and the chill in the air made me sweaty, and I was feeling a little yucky. But maybe I felt bad because I had the wrong attitude. This Olympic champion wanted to invest in me. Didn't I think I was worth it to have the very best? After all, it's a good thing to be pushed to my limits and know that I could go even further and soar even higher.

Taking a deep breath, I said, "Yes. I'm ready to try."

"Good," he said. "For quitting, I want you to give me five laps."

"Five? I only walked on the last one," I complained.

"Yeah, you quit on me, so you owe me that one, plus you got to do the whole thing over. That's five."

I wanted to scream, grunt, and yell but I decided to keep going. I decided that the pessimistic me wasn't going to get the victory.

When I finally crossed the line after the fifth lap, I felt proud.

Coach said, "That's what I'm talking about. See, I knew you could do it all along and now you know for yourself that you can. Most of being an athlete is mental. You've got to be prepared but it's also a matter of the will. Don't give up because you only defeat yourself. Be positive and give yourself a chance to win every time."

"All right, I'm ready for you to make me that champion," I said to him.

"And with that attitude, a champion is what you'll be."

⊰≈⊱

It was Thanksgiving morning and we were headed to church. Uncle John and Aunt Lucinda's baby girl was being dedicated.

"Your dad needs to hurry up and get here," Mom said, as she paced back and forth looking at her watch. "I don't want to be late for the service."

"I just talked to him, Mom," York said. "He's on the way. Relax."

She snapped, "Boy, you better go sit down somewhere. As hard as I work around here, you kids think you can talk to me any kind of way."

Mom was very moody lately. One minute she was smiling and the next minute she was sad. My brothers and I just decided that we'd stay out of her way. Part of me wanted to ask her what in the world was all of the attitude about, but I knew she'd put me in my place so I went and just prayed for her.

When Dad finally arrived, she went off on him, "Where have you been? What took you so long? You know you had us waiting. I can't believe you did this!"

In a calm voice he said, "All right, all right, I'm sorry, Yvette.

There was a traffic jam on the highway. You know I don't want y'all to be late for the service. My brother's all excited about this baby. And my family looks real nice. This is my first Thanksgiving as a free man in a long time. I'm glad to be celebrating around a kitchen table with a turkey dinner and, most of all—my family. I'm ready."

She just rolled her eyes at him, grabbed her purse, and walked out the door. I was left behind to lock up.

"What's wrong with Mom?" York asked Yancy on the way out the door.

Yancy whispered and shook his head. "I don't know."

On our way to the church, Dad's cell phone rang. "Who's calling you on Thanksgiving morning?" Mom asked him.

"Man, she all up in his grill," York whispered to me.

I nodded because I'd noticed the same thing. I thought back to my date with Myrek. When I was in the bathroom for a really long time getting ready, Mom had told me that wasn't necessary. That same evening she also told me she didn't care about Myrek's dad having a date.

But all of that didn't stop her from taking a long time to get ready for church this morning. *Was she falling for my father again and didn't even realize it herself? Oh, that would be just too much to hope for.* I had to dismiss that thought from my mind when my dad started laughing and chuckling on the phone.

"Oh, thank you," he said. "That's so nice of you. Happy Thanksgiving to you. Yeah, I'll be back in Orlando the day after tomorrow. That sounds fine."

Now I didn't know who he was talking to and what the other person was saying, but he was really nice to that person. Both my brothers' eyebrows were raised. What was up?

Mom didn't hesitate; she came out and asked, "Who was that?"

"Just this lady I work with. She's real cool. She wanted to make sure I was taken care of for Thanksgiving and stuff," Dad said nonchalantly.

"What?" I could tell that Mom didn't approve.

She sounded so cute; she didn't even realize that she was so jealous. The three of us just looked at each other in the backseat. Maybe our parents are getting back together for real. Of course, the two of them couldn't see it at that moment because Dad was busy defending the fact that the call meant nothing, and Mom was over the top insisting that it did. I was happy when we made it to the church parking lot so the fussing could cease.

"They're just acting like two married folks," Yancy said to York and me.

I could only imagine it. But all of the thoughts about my parents getting back together faded for a second as I watched them standing with Uncle John and Aunt Lucinda at the altar with the sweet little baby girl, Angel.

With his hands lifted toward heaven, our pastor said, "In this life, troubles will come, storms will rise. There will be mountains and obstacles that will get in her path, but today, this child of God is surrounded by love and family. Those of you at the altar and in the audience—family and friends alike—please join me in telling God you will help her persevere through it all. When she's down, love can lift her. When she's confused, love can help her find her way. When she's broken, love can mend her heart. And when all is good in her world, love can celebrate with her, keep her humble, and let her know that heaven is pleased.

"We are not only thankful for all that God gives us, we are also thankful for God's love. Even this precious baby girl will grow in love when she learns that Jesus died for our sins and gave us everlasting life. Lord, we thank You for this gift of life and we give this gift back to You. May we always be good stewards of Your gifts. Amen." And we all joined in saying amen too.

Later on in the service, the pastor got up again to deliver his sermon. I actually enjoy his messages because they seem so real. Even though I haven't always fully understood where he was coming from, I could always take something from his powerful words.

He began, "You know, I find it interesting that different members of the church have been coming to me complaining about this and that. Yes, I am the pastor and I do intercede on everyone's behalf. I take all concerns and cares to the Lord. But when you come to me about how life isn't fair, you have to understand that everything in life isn't always going to benefit you. Instead of looking for somewhere to place blame when we are not satisfied, we need to look within and just be thankful for what God's already given us.

"If you don't have everything you want this Thanksgiving Day, quit looking at other people and look at yourself. We allow the Enemy to defeat us when we operate out of selfishness. The Word of God says in Luke 6:38: 'Give, and it shall be given unto you; good measure, pressed down, and shaken together, and running over, shall men give into your bosom. For with the same measure that ye mete withal it shall be measured to you again.'"

"It's all right to ask God for something, as long as you ask according to His will. But also ask yourself what you are willing to give. Let me suggest to you to offer a sincere heart to others. Be the bigger person and learn to sacrifice more for the good of others. You will receive according to what you have given. But know that the same is true in reverse. If you give others a hard way to go, what do you think you deserve in return?

"So work harder toward your goals. Dreams can come true. You need to know that God will give you the victory when you give others the gift of love. And, in the name of Jesus, the defeater doesn't win."

Chapter 10

Nurturer
Stays Involved

"Y ou need to move out of my way," Raven said to me as she pushed me, trying to force me across the hallway.

That harsh shove made my books fall out of my arms and onto the floor. For a minute, I just stood there and couldn't react. As I collected myself, I was thinking, *Okay, I just had a great weekend spending time with my family and going to church. We were giving thanks for so much. And as soon as I'm back at school, Raven comes and gets in my face with this drama.*

Then I heard her behind my back getting louder. I mean, when was she ever going to learn to just leave me alone? When school first started she tried the same foolishness and it cost her. Now that Myrek is officially my boyfriend, she's still not able to get over the fact that he really didn't like her anyway.

"Oh, so you don't hear me saying anything to you, girl?" Raven yelled out.

I turned around and said, "Yeah, I can hear you and I'm getting tired of you always starting something with me."

"What, you can't take it?" she said, pointing her finger in my face.

"You better get your finger out my face!" I warned her.

"What you gonna do about it?" she said back to me as her neck rolled to the left and to the right. But she wasn't the only one who could be ghetto. I try to handle myself at school every day with the utmost dignity, but that doesn't mean I don't have street in my bones. She didn't want to go there with me. I had brothers. And I could beat her down if I wanted to. If she kept on trying me, I'd have to show her that she couldn't handle me in no way, shape, or form.

"I'm tired of you spreading rumors about me," she accused.

"What are you talking about?" I was so tired of her nonsense.

"Oh, don't try to act like you don't know what I mean. It's all over MySpace. All my friends have been texting me, e-mailing me, and telling me everything you said."

"First of all, I don't know what you're talking about; and second of all, I don't even get on MySpace."

"Oh, yeah, that's right. I forgot you're too poor to have a computer," she teased. The group that had started to gather was laughing at my expense.

Okay, that was it. She had crossed the line. She might have a bigger house than me, wear brand-name clothes, and get her hair and nails done every week. So, obviously she's used to getting her way, but that didn't mean she was justified in calling me poor. I prefer to be classified as lower middle class because, in my opinion, poor was a state of mind. And because I had a loving family and friends, I was hardly poor. I wasn't out on the street or anything like that. I had just enough to keep me grounded and appreciative. In fact, I believe I'm richer than most.

I was charging up to her with my fist raised and tight. Just as Perlicia and Asia dashed up to me, her girl Shay grabbed her. She was struggling to loose herself. I was fussing with Perlicia and Asia to let me go so that I could tear into her. The next thing we knew, both of us were in the office, and everybody else who had been cheering us on were safely in their classrooms.

"If I get suspended," she said to me before the principal came in to talk to us, "it will be your fault."

"I'm sick of you accusing me about stuff," I said as I stood up.

The principal walked in just at that moment. "All right. Both of you ladies settle down. If you didn't get enough out there in the halls, you're in this office for a reason. Please, don't make it worse."

"My thoughts exactly, sir," Raven said, all fake.

I quickly defended myself. "Please, sir, don't even listen to her. She came up to me and put her hands on me first."

"No, she was in my way as I was walking and I just shoved her by accident. Somebody pushed me into her, sir."

"Okay, now, which one is it?" He looked at us both. "Did you get shoved into her, or did you push her by accident?"

"I don't know. It all happened so fast, but she's making it like I intentionally tried to hurt her or something. I mean, if I was gonna hurt her—she would know," Raven said.

"Uh, that's not true! You can't believe her!"

"Sit back, Ms. Peace. Ladies, listen to me right now. This is not a wrestling ring. This school building is for you to come here and get an education. If that's not what you're about, then you need to stay home or go to another school. I'm telling you both right now if anything else happens between the two of you and you're here in my face, you'll both be suspended. Consider this your warning."

We left the office and parted ways like nothing happened. I was just ready to go home.

I was so happy it was the end of the school day because I was too frustrated to even think. My brothers and Myrek weren't on the bus to drill me about what happened because they had basketball practice. But steam was shooting out of my ears. It took everything inside of me to hold back the tears. And when I got home, I just let it all go.

"Girl, what is wrong with you?" Mom said.

I was so bummed out; I didn't even notice her car in the driveway. "You're home?"

"Yes, and what is wrong with you, Yasmin Peace?"

I ended up telling her the whole story. All the times that Raven had been bothering me from the beginning of school, to her messing with me at tryouts, to her actually putting ketchup on my pants, to her shoving me today.

"Uh-uh. Get in the car right now. We're going right back up to that school," Mom directed me.

"What do you mean? I didn't get suspended yet or anything like that."

"No, but I have an issue with the way this whole thing went down," she said in a fiery tone.

Before we left, she called the doctor's office and said she'd be late to her appointment. It wasn't ten minutes before we were back up at the school and she was demanding to see the principal.

"Mrs. Peace, hello," he said as we walked into his office.

Huffing, yet trying to act civil, she responded, "I'm just gonna tell you right now, I'm not in a really good mood. My daughter tells me that you threatened to suspend her without hearing her side of the story."

"Well, you know you can only believe half of what young people say," the principal said.

"Well, if you would have given my child a chance to fully explain everything, I think you would believe her. What is the website, Yasmin? Tell the man everything you told me."

I gave the principal the site address and he was able to pull up all of the threats that Raven was making against me. Seeing that, Mom was livid. And I felt really uneasy. It didn't make sense that even Raven would try and turn everything around and accuse me of running her down.

"Now, I'm not saying any of my children are perfect, but when they come to this building between eight and three o'clock, then they are your responsibility. I'm telling you right now with the utmost respect, if anybody else lays a hand on my child and you guys don't do something about it, as soon as 3:01 comes I'm calling the police. I'm gonna let them know that you didn't do your job to prevent something from happening."

"I appreciate you coming in today, Mrs. Peace, and caring for your children like you do. Now I see the severity of the situation. Don't worry. I will take care of it," the principal told her.

"Thank you for letting me know that you will," she said before exiting his office and putting her arm around me. "It's okay. Sometimes you just got to stand up for what's right. Never just take the fall for anything without explaining your behavior and telling the true story. If they don't give you a chance, that's what I'm here for."

A week went by and it was time for finals. Everyone was getting excited about the upcoming Christmas break. The last two
months of school were long and dreadful. The workload had gotten more intense, and getting good grades was harder to do. The
last few weeks were crammed with demanding track practices. On
top of that, it was hard to find enough energy to get it done. But
thankfully, I was still able to get good grades and the track coach
was still pleased with my performance. Everyone knew that before
we could enjoy the wonderful freedom of a welcomed break, we had
to pass the finals. And we were all worried about the algebra test.

I was walking to class when Veida came up to me and said,
"You know, Raven's been talking to the other girls on the dance
team."

"And, so?" I responded. "Please don't stress me out right now
talking about that girl."

"Well, she's not happy with you, Yasmin, and I would keep it
from you—but I just don't trust her."

"What do you mean? What are you talking about?" I finally
stopped and listened to my friend.

"She said she's gonna get you in a way that you won't even
know it's her. I wouldn't even know this if I didn't overhear it. She's
always bragging in the locker room to the upperclassmen about
this and that. She never checks the other side to make sure nobody's
in there. She just opens up her big mouth and starts yapping."

"Okay, so what is this crazy plan she's got to bring me down?"

"I don't know and that's why I figured I'd better give you a
heads-up. I just want you to watch your back."

"No worries," I said as I gave her a hug. As soon as I got into math class, my heart started racing. This wasn't good. I had studied for my test, so I was ready, but I had heard it was really hard.

All of a sudden Ms. Reid, our teacher, said, "I've got some really disturbing news."

"What?" a guy in the back yelled out. "No one's gonna pass the test so we don't have to take it?" Then a round of muffled giggles swept the room.

Ignoring the comment, Ms. Reid said, "My exam is missing! I believe someone in this class has it. The test was on my desk when I stepped out in the hallway to make sure all the students got to class on time. When I came back in, it was gone. Everyone, please empty out all your book bags and things right now."

I was the first one to do it because I knew I had nothing to hide. But when I picked up my books off the floor, the guy behind me saw something and yelled out, "Wow, Yas! With good grades like you been getting, I ain't know you had to do that." Everybody started looking over at me.

I was just shocked. "What are you talking about?"

Ms. Reid quickly walked over to my side of the room. She bent down by my desk and picked up the test pages from the floor and said, "Of all people, Yasmin Peace, I'm surprised at you!"

Still in shock, I insisted, "Ms. Reid, that's not mine."

"I know it's not yours, it's mine. It was on my desk, I went out into the hall for a quick second and now I find my missing exam in your possession."

"No, ma'am. I didn't put it there. That's what I'm trying to say."

"We'll straighten this out in the office."

It was always something. Seriously, I was getting tired of that. The teacher didn't act like she was trying to hear anything I had to say. But she also knew I was a good student because I study and work hard. She even helped me after school a couple of times to get the stuff. I didn't need to cheat. My grades are good.

"I didn't do this, Ms. Reid; don't you believe me?" I finally said.

"Again, Yasmin, just save it for the office. Okay? I don't know . . . I get so many kids who struggle in math. It's the brightest ones you never expect to cheat. And I guess an 89 wasn't good enough for you. You wanted to ensure yourself an A, so you stole the test. I don't know. You should have put it back; but since you got caught, you're trying to make excuses."

"No, ma'am!" I said, showing my disappointment that she didn't believe me. I guess the whole explanation theory my mom gave me was not going to get me out of this one. The next thing I know, I was back in the principal's office again. He called my mom on her job and told her everything that had happened.

When he handed the phone to me, Mom said, "Now see, I went out on a limb and told the principal that I know my kids aren't perfect. I said I've got honorable children and here you are now. He's got to suspend you, Yasmin."

"Ma, there's another explanation. I promise you that."

"Just like I told York a long time ago, don't have me go out on a limb for you guys and then I find out later that you did what you're accused of, making me look like some kind of nut."

"Mom, I'm serious. I didn't do it."

"How'd it get there then, Yasmin? Do you have any explanation to tell the people?"

"The guy behind me saw it awfully quickly. Somebody must have put it under my chair."

"I don't know, I don't know." Mom sounded disgusted. "Just

don't get in any more trouble for the rest of the day. We'll discuss this more when you get home."

And just like that, my mother hung up the phone. I knew I was in for it later.

Since I had two more exams to take, they sentenced me to in-school suspension. I just held my head down on the desk. They were going to give me a zero for math because they said I had seen the test. Tears just streamed down my face, like I had dipped my head in water and pulled it back up. I guess the biggest thing now that hurt me so much was that I had let my mother down. Something about my character made her not believe me when I needed her the most. The only thing I could do was pray.

Lord, help me get this all straightened out. I need to ask Your help for my life every day. Right now, I need You badly because You know I didn't do this. How will my mom ever believe me without Your help? Please don't leave me alone, Lord, because I can't handle this alone. Amen.

⌘

"Yasmin, can I come in?" Yancy knocked on the door that night after he got in from basketball practice.

"No, please just leave me alone," I said.

He came in anyway. Mom had told us that we couldn't lock any doors in the house. "What? What do you want? I just asked for some privacy, okay?"

York came in after him. "Did you tell her, man? We gonna get that girl right now."

"What is he talking about?" I said.

"You ain't tell her?"

"I'm trying to . . . but she keeps talking and you keep talking."

"Tell me what?" I demanded.

"Veida came up to me after basketball practice," Yancy started.

"And? She still likes you, you know. You should give her another chance."

"No, no, it's not about that," he said.

"Yeah, girl, it ain't about that," York echoed.

"Well, I'm really not in the mood to talk about anything right now. In case you hadn't heard, I got caught with the answers to the Algebra exam."

"That's what he's trying to tell you," York said.

"What did y'all hear? I know it's all over the school. What did Myrek say? I'm gonna be grounded forever because Mom believed that I did it."

"She ain't gonna think you did no more," Yancy answered.

"Why is that?"

"What we're saying is that Veida knows that Raven girl set you up."

"Huh?" I was all confused at that moment. "She's not even in my class. There is no way that she did this."

"I'm telling you. She did it. She admitted it. You need to call Veida. She's got some evidence or something."

"Evidence?" I jokingly said. "What evidence could she possibly have?"

Then I remembered. I can't believe I hadn't thought about it. Right before I went to class, Veida told me that Raven was planning some big plan to take me down and it couldn't be tied back to her. There was no way I ever would have thought it was her. I went to the kitchen and dialed Veida's number faster than I ever dialed any number in my life. "Hello, hello?" I said before she could even say hello.

"Hello?"

"Veida, it's me. Yasmin."

"Girl, did your brothers tell you? I took it to the dance team instructor. I'm still at the school. You're gonna be completely off the hook."

"I don't understand."

Veida explained. "I told you Raven always runs her yap. When we finished with dance practice, I was on the other side of the locker room changing. You know how slow I am about getting dressed. Anyway, she was bragging about all that she had done to get you in trouble. And I just recorded it all on my phone."

"Are you serious?" I said, not even being able to believe any of it.

For one thing, that I was off the hook; two, that Raven went to so much trouble to get me in trouble; and three, that Veida had taped it all to clear my name. I owed her big-time!

"The principal is supposed to be calling your mom in a minute."

"Veida, girl, I can't thank you enough."

"No problem, Yas."

I hung up the phone with her and called Mom really quickly. She was able to come home and pick me up so we could go back up to the school. Before we got out of the car, she grabbed my hand and said, "I'm sorry."

"It's all right, Mom."

"No, baby. I'm really sorry for not believing you. It's just when they found the evidence . . . and I don't know . . . I'm just sorry. I should have known that you wouldn't have been dishonest like that."

"Mom, more than anything, your trust, your belief in me means so much. I'm excited to clear my name, but for me to restore that trust back in you is even better. I mean, I hope you know that with everything that happened this summer all I want to do is what's right. I've worked hard for my grades. I've really been trying to give myself a good chance to get a scholarship in four years like you've been saying. Colleges look at your grades from the ninth grade on and I'm gonna keep up my good work. I promise, Mom." We hugged.

As much as I appreciated my mother's affection, it was time to handle business. As soon as we entered the school, I saw Raven. But I didn't get angry because she was already being drilled by her mother.

We could hear the lady saying, "As much as I do for you and as hard as it is for me right now, how could you make me have to leave my job to come up here and see about some foolishness! You're mad because a boy chose another girl over you?" Then she took Raven by the shoulders and shook her really hard.

Both Mom and I froze for a minute; we were stunned. I felt bad seeing Raven get into such trouble. Her mother raised her arm up like she was ready to hit her, but then she realized they were in the school building.

"That's the girl, Mom."

"I see, honey. Her mother looks really angry."

"Yeah."

Raven's mom continued. "Life isn't fair, Raven. You're not always gonna get your way, but you're gonna make it harder for yourself if you deliberately try to hurt someone else. Don't you know you reap what you sow? But if you plant good things you'll reap a great harvest in good time."

Then Raven charged back, "Yeah, just like all the good that's happening to you right now? You've been married for fifteen years, and all of a sudden, Dad decides to get a new wife and a new family and just leaves me and you out there in the cold. I don't wanna be like that, Mom. I don't want to lose all the time, and I don't want somebody else to win every time."

Her mother said, "So you just gonna manipulate the system and make it work out in your favor? You know when you lie and deceive it's only gonna be okay for a little while. Pretty soon people are gonna see through your little charade. And because you're out there bragging about it, they saw through it right away. What you did was wrong, Raven. You're such a smart young lady. But to be so book smart, sometimes you do some stupid stuff! And I'm not going to be behind you on it. . . . " Her mother paused. Suddenly, they were startled when they noticed my mother and me walking toward the principal's office. "Is that her?"

Raven nodded.

"You go talk to her right now and apologize to her mother," Raven's mom told her.

Raven just looked at me and started crying. Instead of obeying her mother, she dashed toward the front of the school. I quickly followed her out the door.

I wasn't angry. She was hurt and broken in so many ways. But actually I could feel for her because my own family was just coming together and getting over our brokenness. I had been where she was. I know what being at the bottom feels like, when my dad was in jail and my older brother gone. It's hard to even face the hurt. Mom wasn't able to pay the bills even though she had been working a bunch of jobs and not making a dent in anything. Seeing other girls get all the glory and all the attention made me feel like I didn't amount to anything. So I knew how she felt and I reached out to her.

"Hey, can I talk to you for a second?" I asked.

"I'm sorry. Okay? I really am sorry. I know what I did was wrong and I'm sorry, but you just don't understand."

"I do understand where you are. I know the feeling of being completely broken. And the only thing that made me whole was not a boy, not even my parents, and definitely not money—but God. Somehow, because I've focused on Him, Raven, He has turned things around for me. God is the One you want on your side. God is the One who cares for us and nurtures us—and one thing is for sure—the Nurturer stays involved."

Chapter 11

After
Total Security

I didn't realize how deep the conversation with Raven was going until I could read in her eyes that she was taking in every word I said. Actually, I was ministering to her. I was telling her about how full of joy I was over God's love and how nothing else really made me feel as good as praising Him. And every time I've been through something, His love was the only thing that made me whole again.

"I just don't think He could love me. I mean, my own father could see me every day, raise me from a baby, and just leave me and not love me anymore. So how can I expect some God to love me that I've never even seen?" she asked.

"I'll be the first one to tell you that I'm not a preacher or anything. Besides that, I haven't known God for that long, but He's always known me and He's always loved me. I know when I call on Him, which is all the time because there's always something going on that I need Him there for, He helps me through it. He works things out and makes it better. What else is that but love?"

"It could be nothing else," she said softly. "I guess I've just been so on you because of Myrek. I wanted him to love me but he chose you. But you're saying that even though he's your guy Myrek's not really the one that makes you feel complete."

"That's exactly what I'm saying. But don't get me wrong; I mean, the green-eyed monster got a little crazy and I was jealous for a minute when Myrek first told me he had a girlfriend. I had never even met you and didn't know anything about you. Then, when I saw you at school that first day . . . I was like . . . wow, she is so cute. I really had to pray to get ahold on my feelings."

"You thought I was cute?" Raven said.

"Yeah," I told her. "You are. So I realized real quick that I couldn't make Myrek like me. I also had to admit that my happiness couldn't depend on whether he spent time with me or not. That's when I got on my knees and just asked God to help me."

"So you think that's what I need to do?" she asked.

"I know that it's a personal decision. Jesus says in Revelation 3:20, 'Behold, I stand at the door, and knock: if any [one] hear my voice, and open the door, I will come in to him.' Jesus knocks on the door of all our hearts, but we got to open it up and let Him come in. So you can ask me if you need God and my answer would be yes. I won't say it will make everything perfect, but it's sure great with Him on my side."

"Girl, I want to feel like that," she said in a hurry.

"You will," I assured her. "And from all that you're telling me, you've been at me and making me the bad guy and lashing out because you were hurting. You just need to let Him heal you."

"I remember when you didn't make the dance team. If it was

me I don't even know how I could have come to school the next week. All your girls made it and stuff. I was watching y'all at different times. I checked you out. You said I was cute. Well, I think you really got it going on, Yasmin. Honestly, I know why Myrek picked you over me. You got more confidence and you're just a good choice for him," Raven said, sounding so sincere.

"I don't know if he's good for me or not. I mean, I don't know what'll become of us. But we do care about each other a lot. I don't know . . . we need some time to figure it all out. I just would appreciate if you'd back off, you know?" I was trying to explain to her how I felt about my relationship with Myrek.

"I hear you. Like I was saying before, when I saw you with your friends, you were really happy. And even though you didn't make the team, it seemed like it didn't even matter. I admire how you pushed your bad feelings out of the way. You didn't let that mess up the happiness you shared with them because they had something you wanted. I just couldn't understand how you were able to do that. It makes me think you're a better person than me. Maybe that's why I've been so against you. But now you tell me that it's really about your faith in God."

"Well, I'm not trying to paint myself to be nobody special. I got a lot of struggles too."

"You could've fooled me," she said with a little smile.

Raven just didn't understand. I had been through so much trouble over the last year and a half. And, honestly, not making the dance team was no big deal compared to the changes I'd gone through. But she had to get it; she needed to understand that this whole God thing I was talking to her about was the only thing that carried me through.

I touched her shoulder and said, "I know you're hurting about your dad leaving. I believe he still loves you. He's just not showing it in the way that you want. We can't make other people change. I think that's something that I've learned. When my brother took his own life, I was so angry at him. But he was gone and there was nothin' I could do about it. I asked, why, Lord? You know? But in my time alone with God, He showed me that He's always gonna be there no matter what people on this earth do. No matter how angry we get about stuff that's going on, God will be by our side. If you really want Him to save you, Raven, then get to know Him." All she could do was nod her head and smile.

Then her mom came out to find her. I went into the office with my mother and was cleared from all wrongdoing. Yep, I was glad I told Raven about God because He was sure looking out for me. And that felt great. My mother and I went home feeling relieved. Raven was in a lot of trouble, but with God on her side she would make it through. I felt like I was floating on cloud nine and everything was working in God's favor at the same time.

⬥

"So what in the world are they arguing about now?" York said as he came to my door. Mom was on the phone with our father, and my brother and I were both interested in their conversation. I wanted so much for them to get along and all it seemed like they were doing was not getting along.

Eavesdropping wasn't my style but I found myself trying to figure out what was going on with them. "I don't know," I told York. "She keeps walking from the kitchen to her room, and so I'm getting bits and pieces of her part of the conversation. Who knows what Dad is sayin'."

"All that screamin' she's doing, she needs to chill out," York said. "That's what's wrong with y'all women. Y'all need to just relax and cut a brother some slack. He is tryin'."

"You just asked me what was going on. So how come you don't know that she has a right to be upset?" I said to my brother, knowing that we both have the same agenda. We want our parents back together; however, I couldn't let him beat up on Mom. I know my brother; he has such strong opinions and always takes up for the man's side. And that wasn't cool.

Yancy came out of the kitchen with a peanut butter and jelly sandwich with jelly gushing out of both ends of the bread.

"Ask me what they're talkin' about. I know."

"Yeah, nosy, you would know," York said, trying to snatch the sandwich away.

"You better get in there and fix your own," Yancy told him, as he switched hands to protect his food.

"What is it? Tell me, what are they talking about?" I demanded.

Mom was in her room and we knew it probably wouldn't be long before she came back out again. She was pacing back and forth. That meant she wasn't too happy about something. So whenever she started pacing, we just stayed out of the way.

"Dad wants us all to come to Orlando for Christmas. Mom is completely against it. She wants to split up the time so that he'll have a couple of days with us and then she'd have some days with us. So they're arguing about it."

This was the first Christmas that Dad was free. Jeff was gone. So my family would never be completely whole again. But we'd all

found peace in understanding that it was okay because Jeff was
with God. So now that Dad was out we were as whole as we could
be. Why would Mom have a problem with wanting us all to be together? Why was she holding back feelings I know she felt for our
father? I mean, when he was on the phone with that lady he had
to explain that she was just a co-worker. Why would Mom really
mind if she didn't care for him? York said that last week she had
called him by Dad's name a couple of times. Why would she do
that if she wasn't thinking about Dad?

Yancy told us that Mom had drilled him about what Dad's
place looked like down in Orlando. She wanted to make sure he
wasn't living in a dump. Yeah, it was clear to all of us that she cared,
but for some reason it wasn't clear to her. All of a sudden, Mom
came out of her bedroom and handed me the phone.

"Your dad wants to speak to you. I'm going out to pick up some
chicken, guys. I'll be back." Before we knew it, she had picked up
her keys and purse and was out the door. She was extremely frustrated but so were we. It was an unspoken thing. All three of us
wanted to be with both our parents, and Mom was making it so
difficult. I didn't want to show favorites with Dad, but how could
I hold back the fact that I was angry at her?

"Hello," I said in an uncertain voice.

"It's okay, pumpkin, don't you worry." He could tell how upset
I was.

"I'm sorry, Dad," I said, holding back my tears.

"It's all right. Mom's just gonna need some time. We're gonna
keep praying. Okay? We'll all be together soon."

"Dad, I just don't know what to do. I mean, I want to be with
you for Christmas and I want to be with her too. I don't want to

have to choose and I know the boys don't either."

"I just told you not to worry. It's a good thing both your parents love you, right? We're gonna work through all this. God's got us. Is that your phone?" he asked when there was a pause in the reception. He was right, someone was calling. I looked down at the caller ID and it was Veida.

"It's just one of my girlfriends. I'll call her back."

"No, no, no, you talk to her. Tell your brothers to let me handle this. I know they like to think they're big men but it'll all work out. Go talk to your friend."

"All right, Dad. I love you." I clicked over and said, "Hello."

"Hey, girl," Perlicia said. "It's the crew."

"Hey," Veida and Asia said in unison. "What you up to, girl?" Asia asked.

"Nothing much. You guys really saved me."

"Yeah, we couldn't believe Raven was that crazy," Veida said. "I was just glad I was there at the right time to catch the foolishness on tape. I mean, nobody would even believe I could make up such a crazy story."

"I didn't believe her until I heard it for myself," Asia said.

Perlicia commented, "Well, I believed it. That girl's been psycho this whole year."

"Yeah, but I talked to her and she got issues just like us," I added.

"Ooh, tell us. What's going on?" Perlicia said.

"No, I ain't even gonna go there. I'm just very, very thankful that I have friends like you guys who care so much that you'd spy to get me out of trouble."

"Well, maybe I'll be a lawyer like my dad," Veida said, "because if it doesn't fit you must acquit. And you didn't steal no test."

"What happened to her?" Asia asked. "With all that she put you through."

"For real. All those days they gave you they need to double it for her since she caused all this craziness," Perlicia said.

"I don't really know. I know she's suspended for some time, but I didn't get into all of that."

"See, you just care too much," Perlicia said, a little disappointed.

"No, I just know how it feels to go through trouble. And you guys gave me so much support that now I can feel good about myself. So I don't even want to trip over the small stuff."

"But can we stay friends for the rest of high school?" Perlicia asked. "I mean, is it even possible?"

"We're girls. We're gonna have drama. But we got a deep bond," I explained. "We're gonna be friends way after high school. We're always tight, right?" They all agreed.

❧

A week later, Mom was in a real good mood. "Yas, are you sure you don't want to go with us to the ACC Championship? My boss gave me these tickets. It's gonna be a great game."

"Dad's coming up here, Mom, and I don't want to be gone when he comes. Plus, we'll get to have some daddy-daughter time without the boys here."

"Yeah, but we're gonna be back in plenty of time for you to do all of that. Okay? Why do you think your brothers are going? They know they won't miss their dad. Let's have a good time with just the four of us, you know, out in the fresh air. Y'all have been working so hard with school and doing so many other things. There's been so many activities here and there, including your track practice. I just want us to do something fun we haven't done before."

"Mom, if it was a basketball championship I'd want to go . . . like when you get Final Four tickets, count me in . . . but the ACC Football Championship, no, thanks."

"Well, be sure you lock this door when we leave."

"Mom, I stay home by myself a lot," I reminded her.

"I know. It's just that weird neighbor of ours."

I remembered that crazy man she was talking about. A couple of months ago when my girls spent the night with me, he was watching us. It was sort of spooky. I'd never mentioned it to Mom because I didn't want her stressing out. But for her to say that he was weird too; she'd didn't have to worry, I'd be locking up bigtime. And I knew Dad was coming soon. He'd already called two times to tell me that he was on the way.

My brothers were all decked out and acting all happy because Mom was actually taking them to a state championship game. That was huge for them. So the three of them left feeling like they were on top of the world. And for that I was thankful.

But I started wondering why Dad was taking so long to get to our house. They had been gone for about an hour and a half when I dozed off on the couch waiting for him. I didn't even realize Mom had left the blinds open. When I opened my eyes and saw the man from two buildings down peeking in the window at me, I was really startled. He was the neighbor Mom was talking about, and he looked like he was from some scary movie.

When he noticed that I was waking up, he waved as if that would make me think he was all right. I scrambled to reach for the phone in a hurry, but when I looked back at the window he was gone. Where did he go? Was I just imagining the whole thing because Mom had made me overly nervous? I put down the phone, not knowing exactly what to think. Then I rubbed my eyes, trying to make sure that I hadn't just been dreaming. Just when I was ready to dismiss my scary thoughts, there was a knock on the door. All I could hear was muffled sounds, but it had to be my dad.

"Hey, it's me," the voice said. And since the only person I was expecting was my father, I naturally wanted it to be him. So I jumped up and ran to the door. Without really thinking, I opened it. But I was immediately startled when it was that man again. I was shocked! He sounded like my dad, but I had only allowed myself to be tricked into thinking that it was my father's reassuring voice. Quickly, I tried to shut the door.

"Wait, wait, I just . . . I just wanted to ask you—" He was stumbling around for words and scratching his head. But he wouldn't let me shut the door because his foot was in the doorway. I was a smart girl. I knew how to protect myself. How dumb was I not to make sure it was my father before I opened up the door. I had forgotten that I had just seen this man staring at me. I wasn't hallucinating after all. I didn't imagine it; it was real. And by opening the door, I had given this weird man access to do whatever he pleased with me.

"I'm gonna go get my mom. If you could just move your foot, I'll . . . I'll . . . she'll be right out."

"Your mom and your brothers aren't here, baby. I saw them leave. I just want to ask you if—" Then he pushed the door so hard that the next thing I knew he was inside. My heart was racing faster and faster.

"Sir!" I shouted.

"I'm, I'm, your neighbor from down the way. It's me, Craig. And I just wanted to say that you're . . ."

"Sir, sir, please get out, *now!*" I screamed at the top of my voice, running toward the door. As soon as I opened it my father was standing there. "Dad," I said as I got on the other side of him as fast as I could.

"What's going on, baby? What's wrong?"

"This man—he, he bulldozed his way in the door." My dad went straight up to him, grabbed him by the shirt collar, and threw him up against the wall. Part of me wanted him to scare the man so bad that he'd never bother me ever again, but I didn't want my dad to get into any more trouble. He was on probation and had to make sure he stayed out of trouble.

"It's okay, Dad, it's okay. I'm okay."

"Go into your room, Yasmin, and shut the door," he said sternly.

I did what he said. When I got in my room, I closed the door and got on my knees. I just prayed. *Lord, thank You for getting my dad here. Please help me have better wisdom and be smarter. That man might not have been trying to hurt me, but maybe he was. I don't really know anything about him. It was just so odd; I was scared, he was acting so weird. Thank You. Thank You for keeping me safe.*

Then Dad knocked on my bedroom door and said, "It's me, sweetheart, it's your father."

I was still a little on edge and didn't want to get tricked again, so I hesitated at first. But Dad could tell, so he started singing the lullaby that he used to sing when I was little. Then I flung open the door and fell into his arms.

"It's okay, sweetie, you're safe."

"I'm sorry, Daddy. I thought he was you. Mom told me to be

careful for a reason. She saw him looking around here and I just . . . I don't know. I'm sorry."

"It's okay, you're all right. God got me here just in the knick of time. I love you, Yasmin, and I want to be a part of your life every day so that I can protect you like a father should. I know you're growing up on me, and I'm not gonna be able to keep you from harm forever. But as long as I can, I want to be here for you because you're my baby girl. I can't ever rest until I know that you're not in any kind of danger. It's my job to protect you, and I'm after total security."

Chapter 12

Healer
Provided Love

"Mom, you didn't have to come rushing home," I told her when I came out of the bathroom. She had come home early from the game after Dad had taken care of that scary man who lived in our neighborhood.

I took a shower to get ready for bed so I could relax and quit stressing about everything that had happened. When she saw me, Mom hugged me so tight that I felt like I was gonna choke.

"I'm okay, Mom, really. You guys didn't have to come back right away."

"Where is the guy?" York yelled out like the protective brother he was always trying to be.

"Dad, are we calling the police?" Yancy said.

"Okay, everybody, calm down. Seriously, I'm all right." I insisted but they just kept talking as if I hadn't said anything. Dad explained everything to them, and it suddenly dawned on me that I was truly loved. All the fuss came out of their genuine concern for me. And as much as my brothers wanted to see Florida State win the ball game, as soon as they knew I was in trouble—like Batman and Robin—they were the dynamic duo ready to save the day.

York came over and gave me a hug. "Sis, I'm sorry you had to go through that."

"I'm okay." I tried again to reassure him.

"Naw, really listen to me. I know I've been a little out of it lately." I knew that this was a big deal for York to actually open up his heart.

"You've been through a lot yourself," I softly said to my brother.

"I know . . . but still . . . dealing with Bone going down and everything . . . yeah, but I'm your brother and I'm supposed to protect you."

"You weren't even here. There's nothing you could have done."

"I saw that man looking at you too. I don't know, I guess I should have told Mom and Dad what I thought about it. Leaving you here alone just wasn't cool. I know Myrek is gonna be mad."

"Myrek? Oh, please don't tell him any of this."

"I think Yancy already did. Mom almost hit Mr. Mike with her car pulling into the parking lot like she was flying a jet or something. They wanted to know what was going on and if everything was okay. So she gave them the short version. I expect he'll be over here pretty soon."

"Guys, trust me. I'm all right now."

"Yeah, but what if you weren't? This could have turned out really bad. If that man had hurt my baby—" Mom was close to tears when she cut in.

"Then, I guess that's why we're all thankful."

"Yes, sir, that's the correct address." I turned my attention to what Dad was saying on the phone. "Yes, I do want to file a formal complaint. We'll be waiting, Officer."

"Is Dad calling the cops?"

Yancy had come in from giving Myrek a full report. He answered my question. "Yeah, he needs to. That man needs to realize he can't just walk up in our house anytime he feels like it."

"'This is something else. I always get on y'alls nerves and I'm always trying to get you guys out of trouble. Now you're like all into what's going on with me. The tables have turned for a change. I want you to know that I love and appreciate you guys so much."

"Man," York said. "That was deep."

"Yasmin, Yasmin, you okay?" I heard Myrek coming through the front door and calling out.

"Wait a minute, who is this? Hold up a minute, son." Dad blocked the hallway to stop him before Myrek could head toward our bedrooms.

"Dad, you know that's Myrek," Yancy called out.

"Yeah, Dad. He's straight," York added.

He looked back at me to make sure I was decent. I was standing in my bedroom doorway wearing my pajamas. But I reached for my robe to let my father know that it was okay. But before he let Myrek pass, Dad grabbed him by his collar. I was sure he was going to give him another warning about me.

As soon as my father did that we heard another voice say, "You don't need to grab my boy like that."

Myrek's father had come into the apartment just in time to catch that scene. Dad let go of Myrek and walked toward Mr. Mike. I just put my hands over my face, not wanting to see a confrontation. It had already been a long night. I was still edgy and trying to settle down. At the same time I was feeling sort of happy that my family cared so much. And now, all of a sudden, my state of bliss was interrupted. More drama had come.

Mom saw something was about to happen and quickly stood between the two men. "Mike, you know he was just joking." She was trying to lighten the situation.

"He don't need to joke like that. He protects his kid, I'm protecting mine."

"Dad, I'm okay," Myrek called out as all four of us kids joined the adults in living room.

"You didn't say that he was here, Yvette," Mr. Mike said to her. "I just wanted to make sure everything was cool and nobody was bothering you guys. I'll leave."

"Yeah, I got it under control. You can do that," Dad informed him in a harsh tone.

"Jeffery, you don't have to be rude," Mom said, calling out his behavior. Then she turned to Mr. Mike and started a conversation. She was thanking him for being concerned and assuring him that everything was all right.

Dad just looked at her before he went and sat at the kitchen table. I grabbed Myrek's hand and we went and sat on the couch while Mom talked to his dad.

"Your dad doesn't like me," Myrek said to me.

"I don't know if that's the case. I think it has more to do with maybe he doesn't like your father."

"Yeah, and because that's my blood, he doesn't like me either."

"Well, that doesn't matter because I like you. He wants me to be happy, and I know he'll come around sooner or later and accept that you are right for me."

"Look at him. He's staring me down. Trust me, I don't think he wants you happy with anybody ever. I know that look. My dad used to give it to your brother Jeff when he came over to see my sister. And he definitely gave Bone a hard time, not that Bone cared. But I don't know, I'm just glad you're okay. I just hate that when I come and see you I got to deal with all this tension."

I took his hand and said, "It's not easy when you really feel something strong for someone. We just got to deal with the life stuff that comes up. Remember, we're only in the ninth grade. It'll get better."

"I understand all that, Yas. I just want you to know that I care about us so much."

"I know you do. I guess I'm just saying that we're learning how to have the kind of relationship the Lord will be proud of. But it might get rough and rocky. Even though my name is Yasmin Peace, my life is anything but peaceful right now. Just don't give up when rough patches come our way; let's commit to being there for each other. I guess that will be really cool. Huh?"

He touched my cheek before he stood up and said, "I hear you, princess. Your prince ain't going nowhere."

I smiled as he pulled his dad away from my family and headed for the door.

About thirty minutes later, the police officers arrived. My father and I gave them a complete account of everything that happened. We also asked for a protective order on our neighbor. My parents felt that since Dad had given him a tough warning it should go on record for two important reasons. One, so I wouldn't have to be afraid of him bothering me anymore. The man wasn't able to come within one hundred feet of our house. And two, we didn't want there to be any misunderstanding about what went on between the intruder and my dad. With the order of protection, we were already on record with our version just in case the man tried to come up with a different story.

When the cops left, I looked over at Mom. She was looking at my father with such appreciation in her eyes. It was a look that I actually hadn't seen her give to him before. "Thank you, Jeffery, for being here. Thank you for getting here on time and thank you for saving my baby," she said as she gave him a big hug.

York snatched me up and yanked me back to their room. Yancy was already there. The two of them were plotting. "All right, so we just need to tell our parents what we want. Do we all agree that we want to be one big happy family and let them work out the rest?"

"Mom is not gonna go for that," I told them both. "She already told us that she doesn't feel for him like that anymore."

"Oh, as if her actions ain't speaking totally different than her words. I'm a man. I know these things," York said.

"You ain't nobody's man. You still a boy," I said, as I shoved him down on his bed.

"For real, Yas. York's got a point," Yancy added.

"Oh, you think I got a point?" my tough brother said to the book-smart one.

"Yeah, you got a point, okay? We give each other a hard time, but it's time to stop all that. It's time for all of us to come together and work with each other. I guess we can include Myrek too."

York looked over at me and said, "You think Dad is gonna go for that?"

"I don't know, York. Maybe," I said.

Yancy added, "Come on, Yas. We could let our guard down. We need a father. If Myrek is involved, he might just be a good help. Let's lay all of our cards out on the table and see what we come up with."

When we came out of the bedroom, Dad told us, "Listen, your mom and I are gonna go out for some coffee. You two, y'all got your sister, right?"

"Dad, I'm okay," I reminded him again.

"I'm just saying. I don't want them to think that they can run the hood right now. And I don't want that boyfriend of yours thinking he can come back over here either. The house is on lockdown. Y'all got it?"

"They know how to act," Mom said to him.

He looked over at her and wiped her brow.

"I know. I'm just saying." She smiled.

On second thought, they didn't need our help. It was easy to see that from the way they walked out of the door together. Even though they weren't physically holding hands or hugging or anything like that, we knew they had the kind of connection that parents are supposed to have. They weren't like people who just shared the same children and didn't care about each other. They had a deep concern for each other and it was hard to hide.

The next night they went out again and the Sunday before Dad went back to Orlando they went out again. And then Mom surprised us when she told us that we were going to Orlando for Christmas Eve.

Dad had saved up some money so that he could take us to Universal Studios. We were going to stay in a hotel, eat junk food, and share family time like we were supposed to.

When we arrived in Orlando we checked into the hotel and went straight to the park. It was so cool to be able to see the action behind the scenes, and the rides were really exciting. My brothers and I were having a great time riding together. Dad and Mom either rode together or they just waited for us to come off.

Then something unexpected happened. As soon as we got off the Spiderman ride, Mom said, "Come on. We're going back to the hotel."

"Where's Dad?" we all asked in unison.

"I don't want to talk about it right now. We're going back to the hotel, okay?" The place where we were staying was only five minutes away, but the three hundred seconds it took to get there seemed like an eternity. There was dead silence all over the car. But that didn't stop York, Yancy, and I from thinking, *Okay, Mom, what did you do to make Dad so mad that he couldn't even say bye to us? And why are you making us go back to the hotel and cut our Christmas Eve family trip short?*

York had a look on his face like he wanted to punch the car door. Yancy just kept staring at Mom like he was waiting for her to give him some kind of explanation. I just held my head back with my eyes closed, wondering what was going on with our father. I'm not sure why love has to be so complicated so I prayed, *Lord, You know what we need. You know what my brothers and I want. I just hope that my parents want to get back together too. So, why is this happening? I got faith in You because I know You love us. Could You help us, please?* Then I leaned my head against the window, praying, hoping, and believing that the Lord heard my prayer.

It was a beautiful December evening and Orlando was lit up so pretty. But at the moment none of us were thinking about that. We had other things on our minds.

"I can't believe he didn't come and get us," York said. He was highly upset.

As my two brothers and I waited by the lobby door for Dad to come back, Mom was out walking around the hotel grounds. We didn't know why she took off, but none of us tried to stop her because we were all really upset. Maybe everybody just needed some space to think and cool down. I mean, somehow we sort of felt like whatever was going on between her and Dad was probably her fault. But we couldn't say anything because it was grown folks' business. It was hard to understand why she was being so hesitant about giving him another chance in the first place. It seemed like they were just too into each other for it to be cut off so abruptly. It had to be her who changed her mind.

"I mean, how can Dad do us like that?" York said. "Just because he's mad at her don't mean he has to act like we don't exist."

We were looking out the window when all of a sudden we saw some headlights flashing as a car approached the hotel entrance. My brothers told me to stay put. They were gonna go outside to check it out. Of course, we were all hoping it was Dad.

"I knew he was gonna come back and get us," Yancy said as he jumped to his feet.

"That's not Dad's car," I told the two of them as the car pulled up closer. But they went out anyway.

"It's Uncle John!" York said. "What you doing down here?" Aunt Lucinda was getting out on the other side of the car. The three babies were in the backseat.

When I heard that I rushed out the door too. As they greeted us, Uncle John explained. "Listen, your parents have helped to make our family whole. My brother called me and said I needed to come and help you guys get settled."

"So, Dad called you but he couldn't say anything to us?" York asked, with Yancy and me needing an answer to the same question.

"Here's the key, honey," Uncle John said to Aunt Lucinda. "Go ahead in and start getting the kids settled."

He said to us, "Your dad told us what rooms you're staying in and we'll be right next door."

"We don't need no help!" York said, throwing his hands up in the air like the last thing he wanted was to be around my uncle and his family.

"Your dad asked us to come. And we thought it would be kind of nice for all of us to spend Christmas together," Uncle John responded.

But York wasn't the least bit satisfied and was getting angrier by the moment. "We're supposed to be staying with him. Why are you here and not him?" he demanded.

"Calm down," Yancy said to York.

Now York was furious. "Don't tell me to calm down! This man has always been like a dad to you. But I've always wanted my own father and stood up for him. Not no uncle, not some pretend father, not somebody trying to fill the shoes that my old man is supposed to fill for me."

Then he turned back to question our uncle again. "So I'm asking you, Uncle John, what's up with my dad? We thought Mom ditched him, but he just up and leaves us like this? What? He busted parole? You gotta give us some answers because if it's what I'm thinking—then it ain't cool at all."

"York, just calm down. Let's go inside. You're getting too loud. People are starting to notice. Slow down, son." Uncle John was trying hard to reason with him.

"Don't call me son again, Uncle John." Then backing down a little, he said, "All right, please. I'm not trying to disrespect you, I'm not."

"Well then, don't. I know you're hurt and disappointed. Just go inside and we can calmly discuss all of this."

"You don't know what I'm feeling. You don't know what it's like not to have a father in your life."

"Wait, wait. Don't play me like that. I ain't never had a dad. My dad was dead before I was old enough to say the word. Like you, me and your father let the streets mess us up some, but we've been trying to get it right and to do better."

"Where is he, Uncle John? Do you know how to get to my dad's house? Because I can take the keys and drive myself."

"You ain't takin' nothin'. Boy, get in your room. Now!" Uncle John was getting fed up and finally put his foot down.

He walked with us to the room door and the four of us went inside. Just then Uncle John's cell phone rang. He pulled it out and said, "It's Jeffery—"

Then he handed the phone to York so that he could talk with Dad. "Dad? Dad? Is that you? Look, you need to come over here right now. We need to talk; we need some answers."

Dad couldn't have said much to him because York hung up the phone right away. All he said to us was, "He's comin'."

A few minutes later, I heard Mom calling out for us. When I

walked out into the outside hallway, I was surprised to see my father behind her. "York! Yancy! He's right here! He's with Mom!"

They couldn't move fast enough. "Dad, what's all this about?" York was the first to speak. His eyes were getting red.

"Just about me being boneheaded and wanting to give your mom the world. Then I realized after being in the park with my family for a couple of hours that my pockets don't run that deep. I was frustrated because it tells me that I can't take care of your mom and you guys like I should, so—" Dad tried to explain himself.

"So . . . we still leave together," York finished the sentence his way. "You ain't have to leave us there. And Mom could have told us something. You knew—"

"What?" she cut in and said. "You guys thought I did something? Guys, you're young. It's complicated and your father and I don't even have all the answers. There are things that we want to give to you guys but right now, financially, we can't."

Unable to look at us, Dad said, "And for me, as the man, this is bad news. I haven't been the provider for you all, and it's really been eatin' at me. I pray I'll be able to going forward but, right now, my work isn't steady. So I just thought it best if I didn't mess up your lives anymore. But God reminded me, He's always made a way. It's just that I don't want to let you guys down."

"Dad," I said, going up to my father. "We don't need things, we just need each other."

Uncle John rubbed my dad's back in a loving way and said, "It's getting late. We'll see you guys in the morning. Jeff, you heard your daughter. All they need is you."

Dad nodded. He looked back at me and said, "I apologize to you guys. I'm supposed to be your security. I never stopped loving your mother and there's so many things I want to make up for. It makes me angry—over-the-top angry—that there's so much I can't do.

"But you're right. I can give my heart to her and to each of you. I can let you know that I'm gonna do it right so you don't have to live without me again. I tried to leave you alone thinking you'd be better off, but I couldn't even get to my place without God dealing with my heart and letting me know my place is with my family. And that's what brought me back.

"Sometimes you got to learn to sacrifice and give up some things so that the thing that's most important can survive. And, Yas, you're right, baby. I'm learning that showing love means more than having money. So I'm gonna do all that I can to take care of you all. And, as your mom said, we don't have all the answers. But together we're gonna try to work this thing out." He leaned over and gave her a big kiss.

I looked up at the sky and heard Yancy say that it was Christmas. My gift from the Lord was so precious. My life wasn't perfect, but I had my family. I'd learned that even though stuff can be rough, if love is in your heart you can get through the tough times. I had no idea what would happen with my family, but God had not left us. God gave us each other and it was the greatest gift of all. The Healer provided love.

Acknowledgments

I don't have a traditional best friend. You know—the lady I'd tell everything to and the person my age going through similar issues as me. Actually, I was quite bummed by this when I went to a movie called *Bride Wars*. It was about two best friends who let their own needs get in the way of their love for each other. At the end of the film when they reconciled, I was sad I didn't have that deep connection in my own life. As I walked to my car the tears fell and I prayed. God as always gave me a very strong word of encouragement about love.

So many of us get caught up in the types of relationships we don't have that we forget to focus, work on, and be thankful for the relationships we do have. I am so blessed with several great girlfriends. In different parts of life I have someone close who understands that part of me. I've got my former grade school crew, my college best buddy, my former NFL wives friends, my Delta sisters, my author buddies, my TV/film friends, and my mommy girlfriends. Just thinking about all those people makes me realize I'm still learning how to love them all. My plate with friends is full. And truly my best bud is my husband.

Point is, whatever relationships you have, forever take care of them. If you love everyone as Christ loved the church and gave Himself for it then you'll have a happy life full of wonderful people you care about and who care about you. I'm not saying everyone always has a loving spirit, but as you learn how to deal with people you will understand you can't control them, but you can control how you respond to them. And good friends may not always like each other, but love never fades from the picture. Always feel love from your heart. And if you do, whether from one best friend or many, love will always warm your soul. Here's a thank you to the people who love me.

To my family, parents Dr. Franklin and Shirley Perry, Sr., brother, Dennis, and sister-in-law, Leslie, my mother-in-law, Ms. Ann and extended family, Rev. Walter and Marjorie Kimbrough, Bobby and Sarah Lundy, Antonio and Gloria London, Cedric and Nicole Smith, Harry and Nino Colon, and Brett and Loni Perriman, your staying on me helps me to learn to love being the best me I can be.

To my publisher, Moody/Lift Every Voice, and especially Lori Raschke, your PR help allows me to learn to love telling the world about my stories.

To my 9th grade friends, Veida Evans, Kimberly Brickhouse Monroe, Joy Barksdale Nixon, Jan Hatchett, Vickie Randall Davis and my new family, Tina Crittenden and Angela King, your genuine concern for me affords me the chance to learn to love my faults and get better daily.

To my publicist, Yolanda Rogers-Howsie, your support has blown me away and allows me to learn to love the fact that people do help others just because.

To my children, Dustyn Leon, Sydni Derek, and Sheldyn Ashli, your lives help me learn to love the fact that I work hard for a purpose.

To my husband, Derrick Moore, your unfailing care of our family gets me to appreciate and learn to love your way of loving me.

To my readers, especially those whose lives are similar to Yasmin's, your self-esteem is important to me because it helps me to learn to love the fact that I write to hopefully make a positive difference in you.

And for my Lord, who loves me the most, Your provision is perfect and teaches me to learn to love and focus on You ... for You are enough.

Discussion
Questions

1. Yasmin's father sets clear boundaries for her friendship with Myrek. Do you think the father needed to step in? What does a healthy teen relationship look like through God's eyes?
2. Veida, Asia, and Perlicia make the dance team. Do you believe Yasmin's reaction to her friends making it when she didn't is the correct one? How should you respond when your friend gets something you wanted?
3. York is about to get himself into trouble. Is Yasmin wrong for wanting to go after York? How can you help someone, but not put yourself in harm's way?
4. Yasmin and Myrek argue over their parents dating. Do you think young people should be concerned with their parent's business? What is a teen's place?
5. Shay plays a prank on Yasmin. Is Yasmin doing the right thing by reporting the incident? What is the right way to deal with a person who gives you a hard time?
6. Yasmin overhears her brother York planning to go out of town to make some cash. Do you think she should have kept this in-

formation to herself? Do you believe God wants you to help people not get into trouble?

7. Yasmin's dad moves to Jacksonville for a temporary job. Do you think the mom is right to be concerned? How can you move on and forgive when you are still angry?

8. York is very bummed that his friend Bone is dead. Is spending time with his dad a good way to help him heal? How can we help people cope with their grief?

9. The track coach asks Yasmin to train. Do you think she is right to quit when the training gets hard? What are ways you can encourage yourself to endure the tough stuff that is good for you?

10. Yasmin overhears Shay getting scolded by her mother. Now that Yasmin understands Shay's situation, is she right to give the girl who gave her such drama grace? How can being the bigger person be a blessing to you?

11. Yasmin is home alone and the crazy neighbor bullies his way through the door. Do you think Yasmin handled this scary incident appropriately? What are things to do when a stranger crosses the line with you?

12. The family is having a blast in Orlando and then the dad leaves the fun. Do you feel the reason why their dad walked away was right? How can sticking together help everyone?

The Negro National Anthem

Lift every voice and sing
Till earth and heaven ring,
Ring with the harmonies of Liberty;
Let our rejoicing rise
High as the listening skies,
Let it resound loud as the rolling sea.
Sing a song full of the faith that the dark past has taught us,
Sing a song full of the hope that the present has brought us,
Facing the rising sun of our new day begun
Let us march on till victory is won.

So begins the Black National Anthem, by James Weldon Johnson in 1900. Lift Every Voice is the name of the joint imprint of The Institute for Black Family Development and Moody Publishers.

Our vision is to advance the cause of Christ through publishing African-American Christians who educate, edify, and disciple Christians in the church community through quality books written for African Americans.

Since 1988, the Institute for Black Family Development, a 501(c)(3) non-profit Christian organization, has been providing training and technical assistance for churches and Christian organizations. The Institute for Black Family Development's goal is to become a premier trainer in leadership development, management, and strategic planning for pastors, ministers, volunteers, executives, and key staff members of churches and Christian organizations. To learn more about The Institute for Black Family Development write us at:

The Institute for Black Family Development
15151 Faust
Detroit, Michigan 48223

We hope you enjoy this book from Moody Publishers. Our goal is to provide high-quality, thought-provoking books and products that connect truth to your real needs and challenges. For more information on other books and products written and produced from a biblical perspective, go to www.moodypublishers.com or write to:

Moody Publishers/LEV
820 N. LaSalle Boulevard
Chicago, IL 60610
www.moodypublishers.com